THE WAY IT HAPPENS IN NOVELS

Kathleen O'Connor

BALLANTINE BOOKS • NEW YORK

Copyright © 1989 by Kathleen O'Connor

All rights reserved under International and Pan-American Copyright Conventions. Published in the United States of America by Ballantine Books, a division of Random House, Inc., New York, and simultaneously in Canada by Random House of Canada Limited, Toronto.

Grateful acknowledgment is made to the following for permission to reprint previously published material:
Shannon Keith Kelley, "Room With a View," from About in the Dark, Shaun Higgins, Publisher. Copyright © 1977 by Shannon Keith Kelley. Reprinted by permission of the author.

Library of Congress Catalog Card Number: 88-92173

ISBN 0-345-37369-3

Manufactured in the United States of America

First Available Press Edition: April 1989
First Mass Market Edition: October 1992

For my father, William O'Connor,
and my husband, Douglas Salmon.

With thanks to James A. Michener
and the Copernicus Society of America.

ROOM WITH A VIEW

Outside his window, seasons degenerate
with the incessant bleariness of booze.

Days yawn by, yet he is fascinated
by nothing but his tight rear view

of buildings closeting other buildings
and the rote avenues of escape repeated

against the bricks like locust shells
clinging in death to autumnal trees.

Fearing reminiscence as the only afterlife,
he fears his present life ill-spent.

One day, he imagines, having never seen it,
he will descend the grid outside his view

and like a child's bad dream at last outgrown,
one day be gone.

SHANNON KEITH KELLEY

Prologue

The mailman had a package for Richard Olsen. Vernice gave him the $1.35 forwarding fee and stuffed the small Jiffy bag into the pocket of her uniform.

A buck thirty-five. What a bargain! It cost two dollars to see the early-bird matinee of some foolish movie. Vernice would have paid considerably more than that to see who had written to *this* lost soul.

Richard Olsen had been in the Michael Keep Nursing Home three months and in that time had not received a scrap of mail or a solitary visitor. It amazed Vernice that someone so young and once so famous could end up friendless. Even after all that had happened to him, he was still good-looking in a blond beachboy way. It was just too bad he was so crazy.

During Olsen's first week at Michael Keep, the director of nursing had told the assembled aides that Richard's brain resembled an empty classroom. She pointed to the hastily sketched stick furniture on the portable blackboard and said, "Once there were smiling children in these seats, but the explosion scared them away."

"Aha, aha," Maria Alvarez had muttered, nodding her sleek head back and forth as if this were some sort of revelation. Even then that South American shoplifter knew that, among her patients, Richard was the easiest target for her pilfering. After three days at the home, he didn't have a blanket, a wastebasket, or a soap dish.

Vernice tucked the Jiffy bag under her arm and turned down the green corridor. Richard's room was the last on

1

the left. He never greeted anyone who came in. He was
too busy staring at his window.

"I don't know why you're so crazy for that window,
Richard. The one in the lobby is a lot bigger." When in
Richard's room, Vernice talked constantly. She was afraid
if more than thirty seconds of silence passed between
them, all the children in her brain would scramble away,
and she would become as empty-headed as Richard.

"You got a package." He was still staring at the room's
only window and paid no attention. "Try and curb your
excitement," she said, setting the packet on his bedside
table, " 'cause I got to work on that bedsore of yours
first."

She crossed his legs at the ankles, grabbed the draw
sheet, and pulled him onto his side. "No, no!" he
screamed, more likely in reaction to the coldness of her
hands than to the violence of the motion.

His blond head now faced the bars of the bed's side
rail. "Can't see your window anymore, can you?" she
asked, somewhat savagely. Something about Richard
brought out the beast in people. Vernice pushed his pale
blue hospital gown out of the way and efficiently rubbed
Maalox on the tear in the blue-pink skin at the base of
his spine. "It's looking better," she told him. "We'll
lick this sucker yet." Then she pushed a pillow behind
him and waddled back to the nurse's station for a hair
blower to dry the Maalox with.

Richard used to have a fancy blow-dryer of his own,
but it had disappeared along with his gold razor. This
morning Vernice had shaved him with the plastic razor
she had gotten free with her McDonald's breakfast. Quite
a comedown for a hotshot football player, but she guessed
Richard didn't know any better.

Vernice put the hair blower on high (though the me-
dium setting would have worked) and aimed it at her
patient's bare butt. Vernice was tender with the old folks,
but she liked to hurt Richard a little bit now and then
just to get his attention. Instead the boy just stretched his

lips a little as if enjoying some private joke. The poor crazy loon.

When she was finished, Vernice sat down wearily in the visitor's chair, the only unnecessary furnishing in the room, and one of the few objects Maria had not taken. "Rest your back a little, Richard," she instructed. Not that he had any choice in the matter. Richard would remain suspended on his right side with his paralyzed left arm clamped to his chest like a chicken wing, until she removed the supporting pillow.

Vernice's youngest son was a rabid football fan. Though he could barely read or write, he knew all the teams' statistics: Buffalo, 9–4; Tampa Bay, 2–11. Someday she ought to bring him here and make him look at this mess—Olsen. But hell, she reflected, you couldn't blame football for Richard's stroke. She heard he hadn't been much of a boozer either—just damned unlucky.

"Been worried about my little one, Richard. He's not doing so hot in school. And he sees his brothers coming home from dates at eight o'clock in the morning, and I wonder what he thinks. He don't ask, so I guess he knows. Kids today know everything, but they don't know right from wrong. When I was a kid we didn't know nothing, but we did know right and wrong."

Vernice consulted her watch. In ten minutes she could go home. Then she remembered the package. "We better roll you over, sugar, and check out your mail." She pulled the four staples off the flap of the Jiffy bag and dumped the contents onto Richard's table. "Bubble gum! Lord, Richard. My kids had better than that left over from Halloween."

Olsen did not seem disappointed by the gift. He immediately began sliding the twelve pieces of gum into groups of two.

Vernice looked at the Jiffy bag. It had been forwarded from the McKuehn Rehabilitation Center in New York City, where Richard had undergone physical therapy, but the return address was local: C. F. Freedman, 700 Heritage Square, Ridgely, Connecticut.

"That's not seven miles from here, Richard. You know what I'm going to do? When I get a chance, I'll give your friend a call. I'm not sure if you want company or not, but a visitor sure wouldn't do you any harm. How about that?"

Richard finished dividing the gum into six groups.

"And if this C. F. Freedman is a woman, you know what else I'll do?"

Using his right hand and his teeth, he removed the Bazooka wrapper from one piece of gum, then stuffed the gum into his mouth.

"I'm going to wash your hair. That's what." Vernice leaned over and pushed a strand of Richard's greasy limp hair away from his face.

She had finally succeeded in capturing his attention. He stopped chewing and stared at her, fish-eyed and hateful. "Curses on you, women," he hissed.

"Curses on you, too, Richard," Vernice answered pleasantly, and then waddled down the hallway for her coat. Her shift was over.

Chapter One

For the last two miles of the trip in to Software International, Cheryl used Interstate 84. In the brief space between Route 7 and the entrance ramp, she could see what was left of the old state fairgrounds. The grandstand was still visible but the storybook village—the ceramic statues of snowmen, Santa Claus, and Paul Bunyan—had been torn down. A land developer had bought the property and was preparing to build a shopping mall. Cheryl sometimes felt as if everything familiar was being ripped away. But no, not everything, she thought as she stubbed out her cigarette. Her boss, Mr. Raymond, was dependably predictable.

Mr. Raymond smoked a solitary cigar every morning. Had he known that the smell of it sickened Cheryl, he would have ordered her a slightly more elaborate floral arrangement on Secretary's Day.

Cheryl poked her head into his office. "Good morning, Mr. Raymond."

"Good morning, dear."

His smile was impersonal, theatrical. Cheryl was not fooled by the *dear* either. It simply meant he was preoccupied and could not for the moment remember her name. But he had it right later when she brought him the night's stack of telex messages. "Thank you, Cheryl."

"You're welcome." Cheryl often wondered if Mrs. Raymond asked her husband to describe his secretary what he would say—surely nothing as specific as red-haired, small-shouldered, wide-hipped. No, she was fairly certain he would spread his long fingers apart, pause for a second, then reply: "Youngish."

Cheryl was generally glad for his lack of scrutiny. Though her marriage had been annulled two years before, she had not yet notified either of her bosses and probably never would, since she was keeping her married name. Cheryl Freedman might be taken seriously, but she was sure Cheryl Farrell never would be.

Mr. Raymond finished his cigar with one loud satisfied sigh. It was odd, she thought, that he enjoyed the cigar so much but took no pleasure in the Danish he consumed before it. He ate the pastry quickly and furtively with his back to the door. Maybe he was embarrassed because his wife did not cook him a proper breakfast.

Her other boss, Mr. Derrigo, by contrast, was not embarrassed about cooking his *own* breakfast. Several times she heard him brag about it to coworkers. "Marge," he would say, "does all the cooking at night and on the weekends. But on weekdays she sleeps in and I'm in the driver's seat. So I get out that fry pan and I fry my own egg." It was a terrible eye-opener to Cheryl that a senior manager who signed one-hundred-thousand-dollar contracts and controlled millions in discretionary investment funds was enormously challenged by frying an egg.

But if one remained a secretary long enough, eventually all childhood myths would be shattered. Take, for instance, the myth of the male's superior business acumen. Cheryl was in a position to know that that was perpetrated simply by desk arrangements. Men seated themselves in quiet, comfortable cubicles while their secretaries (usually female) were put at work stations out in the heavily trafficked hallways. A call director was attached to the desk and the constant ringing of these phones guaranteed that the women could not concentrate on any given subject for more than three seconds at a time.

"Good morning. Mr. Raymond's office. Yes, he is.

But he is not at his desk right now. Could I take a message? Okay. Fine. I'll tell him. You're welcome.''

To keep her voice soft, fluid, and nonabrasive, Cheryl took periodic beverage breaks. At ten she bought coffee and then again at three. Each time she fished thirty cents from her wallet, locked her desk, and went downstairs to the first-floor coffee machine, counting in increments of 1.2 as she descended the twelve concrete steps: 1.2, 2.4, 3.6, 4.8. . . . Coffee with one packet of sugar and a heaping teaspoon of Cremora cost her thirty-five calories, but the downtrip sloughed off nearly fourteen calories and ascending the stairs knocked off another twenty-nine. Therefore, the entire transaction left her eight calories in the red.

Despite the caloric advantages of the breaks, Cheryl went for coffee reluctantly. To the left of the coffee dispenser was a refrigerated vending machine with five windows that illuminated the dark hallway like votive candles in an empty church. Behind the top pane today was a large-pored, thick-skinned orange. Showcased in the next three windows were an apple, a container of yogurt, and a sandwich with yellow curling cheese. None of these items disturbed Cheryl. It was the bottom pane with the hot cross bun behind it that she could not so much as glance at without remembering her first football game and how Richard Olsen had looked in his white and gray jersey as he ran across the field, hands on hips.

All through the game she had kidded herself into believing her growing infatuation with Richard Olsen was as innocent as admiration for a sleek cat or a fine racehorse. Then at work she had stared at the plastic-wrapped roll with pounding heart and flaming cheeks and known better. Maybe it was Stu's desertion that had left her so vulnerable. But nothing could excuse her. Later, when she read in the newspaper that Olsen had been stricken with an aneurysm, she felt as if her own foul thoughts had somehow blighted him. Now, carrying her coffee, she passed the vending machine with averted eyes and went back upstairs.

Cheryl set the Styrofoam cup down gently, careful not to spill coffee on the list of frequently used phone numbers taped to her desk. A green plush surface meant to accommodate such reminders bordered the front of her work station. But the green pile surface was soft, flesh-like, and she was unwilling to stick pins into it. Instead, in direct defiance of corporate directives, she Scotch-taped all memos to the face of her desk.

"Cheryl."

Mr. Raymond was back in his office. "Yes, Mr. Raymond."

She put down her cup. The coffee was just right—hot but not steaming. In five minutes it would be tepid and tasteless. She wished just this once Raymond would come to her. Instead he began mumbling and she was forced to walk into his office. "I'm sorry, Mr. Raymond. I couldn't hear you."

He was reclining backward in his executive chair with a set of plane tickets on his lap. He displayed the bottom ticket. "Coming back, Travel has booked me tourist."

Tomorrow he was going to England, and she could catch up on her filing. It would be a vacation of sorts. Cheryl eyed the blue and green ticket. "Yes, that's right. Going over you're on Pan Am and they have a business-man's class. But you're coming back EurAir and they don't offer that service."

"That was all Travel could book me on?"

"I'm sure." She was not in a position to challenge the Travel Department's decision. If Mr. Raymond wanted to tackle Travel, he could. She doubted he would. Raymond was a bully only to his wife and secretary.

Sure enough, he shook his head and said, "That's all right. It's not that long a flight. Not like I'm coming back from a symposium in Russia."

Cheryl nodded and backed toward the door but halted

when Raymond asked, "How's your work going? Everything all right?"

"Fine." Men had underestimated their own loneliness when they had designed these private cubicles. When his phone was not ringing and subordinates were not dropping in, Raymond often appeared at the side of her desk and asked if her work needed what he called "prioritizing." She required no such assistance but would obligingly hand him a sheath of papers to rearrange so he could spend a few minutes standing beside her.

Today she couldn't provide solace. A phone was ringing and her coffee was getting cold. "Mr. Derrigo's office. No, he's out of town. Could I help you?" A message began clattering in on the telex: *rat a tat tat. Ba de boom. Ba de boom.* Raymond's phone rang and then his overflow line rang. The signals on the call director flashed like miniature Christmas tree lights. ". . . Yes, he is, but he's on another line right now. Can he return your call?"

Cheryl looked up as the mailboy noisily dumped an armful of mail into her in box, then lifted a large box from his cart and left it precariously tilting on the ledge over her desk. The box blocked her view, so she slid it down to her desk and then onto the floor. If Mr. Derrigo were in and unengaged, he might have emerged from his office to assist her. But he was visiting three branch offices on the West Coast. Last Friday he had asked her, "You know how to reach me?"

She had managed to nod without smiling, though the question amused her. She had made all his travel and hotel reservations, booked two hotel meeting rooms, and arranged a banquet for him. But in his mind such arrangements took care of themselves in the same magical way that coffee, doughnuts, and lined pads always appeared in his conference room at the beginning of staff meetings.

At 12:30 Cheryl carried her brown-bag lunch into Mr. Derrigo's empty office. His desk was bare except for a marble-based pen set and an old photograph of his now college-age children in parochial school uniforms. She spread out a paper towel and pulled out her sandwich and diet soda. She used to eat her lunch in Software International's makeshift cafeteria of folding tables and microwave ovens, but avoiding the greasy food and pretending to be married in front of the other secretaries became too much of a strain. Nowadays she took her brown bag and a Regency romance novel down to whatever office was vacant.

Though she read fiery contemporary romances at home, Cheryl felt Regency novels were more subdued and better suited to the office. Through Derrigo's closed door, she heard the soft, intermittent hum of an unanswered phone in the distance, but she did not stop reading. As a secretary of six years, she had lost the anxious-to-please intensity that required her to answer all phones—along with the belief that she would be rewarded for doing so. Nothing would change.

She was also not in the least threatened by the new word processing center. No production typist would be able to decipher Mr. Derrigo's abbreviated scrawl or comprehend Raymond's acronyms. But sometimes she wished a machine would be invented that could perform her entire function. No one should spend a lifetime doing what she did.

Infinitely more appealing were the contretemps that occupied the heroine of *Heart's Masquerade*. Lady Waverly, resisting pressure to marry, was on the lam, dressed as a man and riding in a stagecoach. Her driver, a fair-haired member of the gentry, was disguised, for reasons undisclosed, as a peasant. But Cheryl knew what would happen. She often imagined that the heroines of these novels possessed her own type of moist-eyed, puffy prettiness, and she endowed the heroes with Richard Olsen's athletic handsomeness.

Olsen had been an attractive man, but with a regularity of feature and a lack of menace that prevented him from

achieving sex symbol status. Cheryl had always been relieved about that. But she was grateful to Olsen for more
than his good looks and accessibility. He had helped her
develop standards.

On the night she attended her first football game, she
felt like a failed woman, one without a meaningful relationship. After her breakup with Stu, she had joined singles' organizations, pen pal clubs, and allowed boring,
unattractive losers to press too close and demand,
"What's wrong with you?" or "What are you afraid of?"
Then she watched Olsen bound gracefully across the field
and immediately she felt less impoverished. She decided
she would either date someone like him or go without.
And going without proved to be not all that difficult—not
much different from dieting. It was just a matter of sub-
stitution. She began staying home and reading romantic
fiction. The novels might be a diluted substitute, but they
were safe and spared one the cold, grimy feeling of single activities.

It was soon after that the idea of the bubble gum came
to her. It was a way of conveying—anonymously—a to-
ken of her esteem and affection for Richard Olsen. There
was also a kind of excitement and awesome finality in
standing to the other side of the Elgin Avenue mailbox
and knowing that she, a passive, indecisive person, had
just completed an absolutely irreversible act and that no
amount of plunging of her freckled arm could retrieve
that small Jiffy bag.

But Richard Olsen had taken sick and sunk from public
view as completely as a stone thrown in a pond. And
now there was only the vicarious excitement of the novels. At 1:30 she slammed the book closed. From reading
so much she had begun to apply a fictional narrative to
her own life and as she stood, she stated softly, "Cheryl
Farrell Freedman returned to her desk with a solemn res-
ignation."

As soon as she left the solitude of Derrigo's office, she
dashed to answer a phone. "Mr. Raymond's office. He's

at lunch, Mr. Krupa. This is Cheryl. Could I help you
with something? Hold on. I'll get the file.''

At five o'clock her lipstick-stained second cup of coffee was still three-quarters full. She tidied her desk, covered the typewriter, clicked off her desk light, dumped
the undrunk coffee in the hall water fountain, then threw
away the cup in the ladies' room. Martha Austin, a secretary from the Marketing Group and a newlywed, stood
in front of the double mirrors carefully combing her long
blonde hair. Cheryl did not pull out her own comb. She
was not going home to anybody. "Good night, Martha."

"Good night, Cheryl."

Cheryl was relieved it was a Thursday, and she was
not required to say "Have a nice weekend" and answer
Martha's inevitable question, "Big plans?" The older she
got the more repetitious her conversations became. She
smiled at Martha and went out to her car.

The car, a vintage Vega, was very dependable, thanks
to Al Valerino, her stepfather. Her mother had remarried
only a few months earlier, and, at first, Cheryl had been
looking forward to Al's joining the family. The swarthy,
muscled, sometime carpenter and school bus driver was
just ten years older than she and could never be a father
figure; but she had hoped he would prove to be an ally
in the alien world of men. And though she did not want
her mother's new husband to be interested in her, she
had hoped he would find her interesting. Instead Al
viewed her as a disintegrating mess, like Jell-O left too
long at room temperature. All her topics of conversation
pained him. He did not want to know any details of her
brief failed marriage with Stu or hear her reminisce about
her dead father. So when he and Rose occasionally came
for drinks and dinner, to avoid small talk, Al would first
check the upstairs pipes, then go out and inspect the car's
battery and spark plugs. If it was a long drawn-out holiday dinner, he would change the oil. Right after the coffee was poured he would excuse himself by saying,
"Giving you ladies some time for girl talk," then, still

carrying the white fluted cup, he would go outside and set to work. Though this strained relationship was hard on her ego, her car ran like a top.

When Rose married Al, she had given Cheryl the condominium, which was set in a row of attached two-story houses with similar though different-colored fronts. Tonight, when Cheryl emerged from the car, a neighbor, wheeling a baby carriage on the bit of sidewalk adjoining their homes, smiled appealingly at her. Cheryl waved and was on the brink of saying "Nice now that it stays brighter in the evenings," when she remembered that the woman was from Quebec and spoke no English. She waved a second time and went inside.

Having decided on chili for dinner, she began dicing an onion and a green pepper. The knife made a savage sound as it hit the porcelain cutting board: *Screw Al, Screw Stu, Screw Mr. Raymond.* The onions hissed as she dumped them into the too-hot frying pan. She threw out the last bit of green pepper rather than tangling with all those seeds. Her mother would not have been so thriftless. No, she would have hacked the skinny green slice free and frozen it. Now Rose, the most economical person Cheryl knew, lived with a man who had never held a full-time job.

Right after dinner Cheryl headed upstairs, looking forward to finishing the Brushfire romance she had begun the night before. She started counting in increments of 1.2 as soon as her foot hit the bottom step. It occurred to her that such constant involuntary caloric computations were nearly as handicapping as a facial twitch. But she could not stop. An unchallengeable mix of vocation, habit, and disposition made her always listen for phones and count calories.

Cheryl had left off in the novel with the hero and heroine drinking an amber colored liquid; she wished the writer had just named the beverage. The novel was full of coincidences and foreshadowing but nothing truly upsetting. Just as the couple were getting amorous the downstairs phone began ringing.

Cheryl bounded down to the kitchen, not counting calories but orienting herself. She need not answer "Mr. Raymond," "Mr. Derrigo," or "Software International." She was at home. It was probably her mother. "Hello" would be sufficient.

"Is this C. F. Freedman? This is Vernice Johnson. I work at the Michael Keep Nursing Home on Birch Lake Road."

A fund-raiser, Cheryl cautioned herself. She decided to pledge no more than fifteen dollars. That's what she had given the Police Athletic Association.

"You sent a package to Richard Olsen?"

Cheryl thought of the package of bubble gum stored in her desk at work. It had been months since she had sent any to Olsen. She had stopped not because he was sick but because she no longer had a current address for him. "I mailed that last one a long time ago. To a rehabilitation center in Manhattan." Then she added: "It was his trademark when he was playing—the gum, you know."

The woman did not seem to know. She sighed. "God love the U.S. mail. He's lucky it was forwarded. He's been here about three months. What I wanted to ask is: do you want to come and visit Richard? Those that get company get better care."

Cheryl flushed. For over a year she had entertained the fantasy that when Richard Olsen had his comeback conference, she would be tight by his side, smiling proudly. "Does he want to meet me?"

"He doesn't know what he wants. But like I said, those that get company do get better care."

Cheryl felt as if an ice cube were slowly sliding down her spine. The woman was saying that Richard was both abandoned and a vegetable. There was never going to be a press conference.

"Why don't you come around noon tomorrow: Birch Lake Road. I get off at three."

Derrigo was on the Coast and Raymond would be in Europe. She could take a long lunch. "All right."

She hung up the phone. Unwilling to imagine what lay ahead, she walked back upstairs and reread the last sentence on the page where her bookmark lay.

Her eyes blazed like diamonds.

Instantly Cheryl realized she was no longer in the mood. She should have gone swimming at the YWCA or performed other activities that burned up calories. Disgusted, she stared at her idle hands.

Richard used to stare at his hands, too, when the pass was high or underthrown. Though she had only attended that one football game, she often read about him in *The New York Times*, where he would be pictured with his dog, Heinz, or his girlfriend, fashion model MacLogan Ross. And you could tell by that interchangeable, thoroughly fabricated name what kind of a woman she was. Ross was soft and easy to say; so of course, the model had chosen MacLogan, which required both a forward and backward thrust of the tongue to pronounce, as her first name.

MacLogan was long gone now. And tomorrow Cheryl would meet Richard Olsen herself. She had intended that to happen, but only after she had lost twenty pounds and he had recovered. Certainly not now—not like this. Nothing was working out the way she had planned.

Chapter Two

The women had discovered a new instrument of torture. After Vernice rubbed cold, greasy slime on his backside, she would tease and threaten him with a blowtorch. All that heat directed at his exposed ass reminded him of those Daffy Duck cartoons he had watched as a kid, where Daffy was always getting his tail feathers singed or blown off by dynamite kegs. For all Richard knew, his own rear end might have become feathered and downy. It was part of his anatomy totally lost to him now.

Vernice switched off her machine and ran her freezing cold hand down his crack. (The women always chilled their hands before touching him.) "This bedsore is looking better, sugar. Like I been telling you, we'll lick this sucker yet."

They had already licked this sucker. At the beginning he had vowed to fight to the death. But it was taking too damn long. Even now if a chunk of plaster fell out of the ceiling and landed on his head, Vernice would not let him slip away. No, she would thump him on the back to force the dust from his lungs, then keep him awake in case there was concussion. The women wanted him to live and suffer more.

"Lift your good foot, Richard."

He lifted nothing but watched as Vernice pulled slippers on his faraway feet. The yellow slippers meant the Indian was coming. Richard did not know if the orderly was truly an Indian, but he was moon-faced and resembled the Seminoles who sold stringed beads and skirted dolls at the orange groves where he had worked part-time as a high school student.

After the Indian had him sitting in the wheelchair, Vernice pushed him into the bathroom. First, she threatened to strangle him with a towel; then she poured cold water on his head.

"I told you if your visitor was a woman, I'd wash your hair."

"Help. Help." Richard no longer bothered to raise his voice. He had lost all hope of help.

Vernice had done a bit of maneuvering so he would face the wall instead of the door. Richard knew she did this so he could not peek out and see his window. She had troubled herself unnecessarily. By now he could conjure up the window at will and superimpose it on any flat surface.

The window had twelve panes—three across, four down. He had consecutively numbered the panes beginning with one in the upper left-hand corner and ending with twelve in the lower right. The sum of these numbers was seventy-eight. The totals of the numbers on the three vertical rows were: 22, 26, 30. Horizontally they were 6, 15, 24, 33. And both totals were always seventy-eight.

The paneless picture window in the sitting room, where they dumped him every morning, was no good. It overlooked Birch Lake; he and the old folks were supposed to be content spending hours staring out at that dirty pond.

Today after Vernice left him there Richard managed to get one brake off his chair so he could twirl around and face the other way. The lady in front of him tried to do the same and, when she could not, began to cry. Instead of lifting the brakes, her veined hands moved up and down picking lint off her nylon bathrobe. "She wants to be moved," Richard told the nearby volunteer. The pink-jacketed lady volunteer, startled by his unaccustomed garrulousness, flinched but made no move toward the old lady.

The side of the woman's chair was stamped with a
cellophane logo containing the name Everest & Jennings.
Everest Jennings, Richard thought, would be a good name
for an American explorer, an Admiral Peary type.
MacLogan Ross had been a good name for a model. As
good as any.

She probably did not need to work anymore. Perhaps
after offering him as a victim she would have been allowed to retire to some Palm Beach hideaway. Though
he doubted Logan would want or enjoy that much. She
wasn't high-class enough to consider privacy a privilege.
Still, she must have received something for her sacrifice.
He wasn't too curious about her compensation. He wondered why she had done it.

Their last night together she had left in a huff. An hour
before that they had been sitting in the living room drinking sherry—the expensive kind. Now, in an effort to remember the brand name, Richard dragged his left arm
toward him and began massaging it. That did not jog his
memory, just caused an uncomfortable tingling in the
dead hand. He looked at the ragged-edged blanket on the
lap of the sobbing old woman facing him and remembered that the sherry was called Dry Sack.

Even though MacLogan was at her sexiest that night,
with shirt open, it had not been a romantic finale. All
they had been able to hear was the click, click of the
dog's toenails hitting against the tile floor of the bathroom above them. Heinz, always jealous of MacLogan,
in a few more minutes would have ripped down the
shower curtain. To avoid that, Richard went upstairs on
a mission of canine comfort. When he came back,
MacLogan was gone.

He had been relieved she had left. His head ached so,
he wished he could remove it, like a screw top, and set
it across the room. MacLogan must, he realized now,
have driven directly to the place (a draft board of some
kind) where helpless victims have their lives signed away.
Maybe she had heard an advertisement on her car radio.

Who knew? He had never known such barbarous practices existed.

He had not even known it when he was lying on the
emergency room table, and some damn fool doctor was
asking him if he had ever been able to use his left arm.
Three days later those lady physical therapists were dragging him around, and he still did not know. It was a full
seventeen days before he realized he was the sacrifice,
the man offered to the women for torturing.

That was the day someone announced he had not had
a BM since his stroke. Hospital people used more acronyms than football coaches. By that time he was aware
that he was a CVA (cardiovascular accident). A CVA seventeen days without a BM. The information passed from
LPN to RN and that afternoon a tight-lipped, broad-assed
blonde with a peaked cap came in and pushed him on his
side. He heard paper crinkling and then with no warning
she forced what felt like a fire hose up his rectum. He
screamed for help. When none was forthcoming, he asked
the blonde if there was a lot of blood.

"You're all right."

People were always telling him he was all right when
he knew, for a fact, that he was not. Though the nurse
had pulled the curtains closed, underneath, not three feet
away he could see a pair of men's slush-stained shoes.
He called to the man, "Help me, sir. Help me, please.
For God's sake, help me." The shoes backed away. That
was when Richard recognized incontrovertibly that he
was the sacrificial offering.

In his freshman year at Iowa, he had been required to
read a short story called "The Lottery." The idea of an
annual stoning had horrified and upset him. Maybe he
had been upset because he had subconsciously suspected
that the practice of human sacrifice still existed and horrified because he sensed that he, too, would have backed
away from the victims.

Vernice walked into the sitting room and laid an icy
hand on his forearm. "I'm taking him back to his room,"

she said to nobody in particular. Even though it was still winter, Vernice never wore sweaters. Richard knew she let her brown arms dangle bare out of short puffed white sleeves so he would always be chilled by her touch.

Maria, the chipmunk-cheeked one, wore thick white sweaters and never paid much attention to him. But now when he was looking forward to moving, she appeared. "It's not time," she said authoritatively.

Vernice pulled his left brake off and glared at Maria. "Richard is having company. I want him to eat lunch and relax in his room first so he'll be sociable."

"Richard is never socie*eee*able."

Vernice was moving him anyway. He was not going to ask her about his company. He would not give her that satisfaction. Though halfway down the hall, he was tempted to wave his arm in a wide looping arc and scream like that game show master of ceremonies: "Come on down. Come on down." Instead he kept his arm tight by his side. Any display of enthusiasm was dangerous.

Once they were inside the room, Vernice did a mean, vicious, nasty thing. She pushed his chair up against the bedside table so that the table's crossbar was between his wheels. He was locked in place like a raccoon with its leg in a trap. Then Vernice set his lunch tray in front of him, lifted the metal cap off the plate, and announced, "Beef stroganoff over rice."

Richard was skeptical. To him the congealed mess looked like muddy Birch Lake frozen over with snow around its sides. The salad looked inedible, too. When Vernice had her back to him, he started to eat the strawberry ice cream. She turned when she got to the door, gave him a look of pure disgust, and said, "No wonder you are always bound up." Nothing he did ever suited Vernice.

After he was finished the nurses generally left him for a long time to stare at the unwanted food on his plate. But this time before he could even begin to count the kernels of rice, Vernice was back to release him and wipe his face. "Got to get you tidied up," she said. "There's a lady coming to see you."

A lady! He tried to keep his disappointment from .showing. He did not want Vernice to know that at this point in his persecution, he was still lunatic enough to hope for something better. He pointed to the bed. "I need to rest for the company."

"Lord, sugar. There's no time for that. You can rest all night." Then she patted his shoulder. "You really do listen sometimes, don't you?"

She had no idea how much he listened. How damn tired he was of hearing about her delinquent kids.

Vernice took his tray, and he heard her smack it down on the cart in the hallway. In a few minutes she returned with a pale, matronly red-haired woman, wearing a camel hair wool coat belted at the waist, and though he found it hard to judge anymore, she appeared to be short. The redhead approached him, dipped her head nervously, transferred her purse strap from hand to shoulder, then extended her hand to him. He shook it. This politeness visibly amazed Vernice. He could not understand why. He had been shaking hands with the opposition all his life.

The woman bent down again, looked him full in the face, and asked, "How are you feeling?" He found her intense gaze unnerving. When he did not answer, her sad eyes began to scrutinize him all over. He supposed he had done the same thing to Heinz, when he had first seen the sick mangy mutt at the pound. He wondered where Heinz was now.

Richard gestured to Vernice for a tissue, but she was too busy telling the woman, "Them with strokes cry real easy; it doesn't mean anything."

The woman pulled a pink Kleenex out of her shoulder bag and handed it to him, then Vernice began steering her out of the room. At the doorway the redhead bobbed her head again, birdlike, and said, "Goodbye, Mr. Olsen."

Mr. Olsen! Good Lord. Nobody had called him that since he had lectured at the grade schools on the importance of physical fitness.

After she left he stuffed the pink Kleenex into his left fist. Vernice found it there two days later when she was bathing him. "Aw, Richard. Don't tell me you're sweet on that redheaded girl. You should've been nicer to her. Maybe she'd've come back."

He was tempted to bite her. Instead he just snarled, "Curses on you, women."

Chapter Three

The place exhausted her. As soon as the heavy glass doors closed behind her, Cheryl began to yawn. She slumped against the elevator railing on the short trip upstairs. Once she emerged onto the third floor the flickering lights of TV sets in the individual darkened rooms began to make her head ache. But as she got to the end of the corridor, the lethargy lifted and her heart began to pound erratically.

Richard's room, the last on the right, was slightly darker than the others. He had no TV set, and the only illumination was a reading light attached to the hospital bed.

"Hello, Richard. How are you?" Though Vernice said he was capable, Richard never spoke; so further inquiries were unnecessary. Cheryl moved to her usual spot, the heat register under the window. The brown paint around the vents was chipped away, and though it was a cool evening, no heat was emerging. Cheryl could not tell whether Richard was cold or not. His face was stiff, inexpressive. The sheet and white-knit blanket reached to his abdomen, leaving his chest and shoulders covered only by a bedgown printed with small blue snowflakes. She quickly looked away because something about those snowflakes caused an ache deep in her chest.

She chipped a bit of the peeling paint with her fingernail and watched the brown splinters fall down the vent. Her legs ached and she wanted to boost herself up on the windowsill, but that would have looked too undignified.

She turned slowly as if asked a question and said softly, "Maturity is knowing when a man calls you *Honey*, it's because he can't remember your name." This was her third visit, and each time her performance for Richard Olsen was different.

Tonight she was the cynical secretary, Mary Berrill—the heroine of her latest Brushfire romance, *Love Conquest*. She lit a cigarette, then quickly stepped forward and stubbed it out in the coffee saucer on Richard's bedside table. She had read somewhere that stroke victims were likely to have respiratory problems. Maturity was knowing when not to smoke.

Though Cheryl immediately moved back to the window, she kept glancing at the bedside table. It had been shoved away from the bed and the dinner tray on it had slid perilously close to the table's metal edge. The completely untouched food on his tray reproached her; if there was anything truly charitable about these visits, she would try and feed him something instead of just babbling on like a would-be actress in an empty theater.

Richard was dangerously thin, and this had altered the contours of his face. In the newspaper photographs, his big boyish grin had always dominated. But now he was unsmiling, his cheeks were hollowed, and the athlete's broken nose became his most prominent feature. The hooked nose combined with the togalike bedgown and straggly blond hair made him resemble the intense young Roman that Cheryl remembered from her eighth-grade ancient history text.

But Olsen was only aristocratically handsome from the distance of the window. Step a few feet closer and he was simply cadaverous-looking. Deep indentations had formed in the skin around his lower neck and some crusted milk had collected in the well under his Adam's apple. Apparently he occasionally took some nourishment. But not much. Not much. She should really try and feed him something. It was her Christian duty. She moved two steps closer to the bed. Richard remained steadfastly staring at the window, oblivious of all her movements.

On his table, behind the small institutional tissue box and to the right of his dinner tray, she noticed a long-necked, Grecian-shaped plastic jug. Though she had never seen one before, Cheryl instantly knew this was a man's urinal and retreated to the safety of the window. She should never have come. It took a special talent to visit someone this sick, and she did not possess it. The breezy blonde matchmaker at One Plus One Dating would have been good at this. It must take the same knack to deal cheerfully with the socially desperate as with the dying.

Dying! Was he really dying? Vernice had hinted that unless he soon took an interest in food or began to co-operate with the staff, complications were inevitable. But if starvation or dehydration was imminent, why wasn't someone on the staff assisting him with his dinner? Perhaps they were encouraging him to be independent? No. He was too ill for it to matter.

She really should try and feed him something. She pushed herself away from the window with the same reluctant arm motion she used to force herself into the pool at the YWCA. "Break a task into manageable portions," the instructor at Software International's time management class had advised. Cheryl decided to go as far as the vinyl visitor's chair and just sit down.

The chair was slanted back and so low that she had a restricted view of the bedside table and Richard's midsection. She glanced at the urinal again and knew she could not feed him. If only Stu and her mother had not insisted on that annulment. (Neither wanted her to be burdened by a marriage that never was. They both wanted her to be free. But free for what? To be as purposeless as a leaf in the wind?) Still married, she might have clung to her Catholicism with a stoic dignity and been nearly a saint. Because Stu had so conscientiously filled out the forms requesting an annulment, she was now free, a wishy-washy woman unable to help a dying man.

Wounded by this self-indictment, she stood, walked rapidly to the bed, balanced a bit of the tuna noodle casserole on a fork, and held it in front of Richard's mouth. When he did not respond, she set the fork back on the tray, and said gently, ''Is it too cold now?''

Richard had not acknowledged her presence since that first noontime visit. Perhaps he felt safer when Vernice was with them. The aide had cautioned Cheryl not to be overly encouraged by his handshake. But she had been sure Richard sensed her sympathy and would open up as soon as they were alone. What a naive soul she was to think a prior relationship based solely on the receipt of bubble gum would call him back to life. ''Touch him and he'll curse at you,'' Vernice had warned.

At the time Cheryl had not believed her, had thought smugly: *oh no, not at me.* Now she knew better. In fact, she almost welcomed the curse; as soon as he did snarl at her, she could go home, conscience free, to her book and never feel obligated to come back.

But where to touch him? She surveyed his hands. The left arm was bent at the elbow with the wrist humped upward. The hand was asymmetrical and ugly, but Cheryl felt if she touched him there the gesture would signify she was more than just a fair-weather friend. Sure, she had worshipped him in his hero days, had obsessively dreamed about him rather than grieve for her miscarried marriage, but she was still willing to be his friend. If he cursed at her now, she could leave knowing he was the one who had done the rejecting. That was important. Even though her mother and stepfather might consider her a perpetual child, she would know that in this one desperate situation she had done her adult best. Cheryl poised her hand over the bloated fingers and quickly went . . . *tap*. Nothing. Then she flushed with embarrassment. Richard probably had no feeling in that stroke-affected arm. So much for symbolic significance. She gently applied her perspiring fingers to his right wrist. His knuckles were the size of walnuts, and for a second she felt pure quaking physical fear. Even in this weakened state he could probably kill her. She applied more pressure to the wrist. When nothing happened, she slowly lifted his hand and decided never to call herself a coward again.

Richard remained silent and inert. But when she looked into his face, Cheryl noticed that his eyes were slowly shifting from left to right. He appeared to be counting the panes in his window. If it took him that long to count twelve panes, his brain was as far gone as Vernice had implied.

"You like to count, Richard? I do, too. I'm always counting calories."

"Calories?"

Whomp! She dropped his hand and stood there terrified. It was as if a face in a familiar painting had begun to speak. There was nothing parrotlike about his voice either. No, it was loud and clear. Cheryl cleared her throat, tried to compose herself. "Calories—you know, in food."

Slowly he turned toward her. His hair had looked curly in all the newspaper pictures but constantly lying in bed must have flattened it. "You been on planes?" he asked.

"Airplanes? Yeah, a couple of times," Cheryl answered in her soft, pleasant phone voice, pretending there was nothing extraordinary about this conversation.

"You know those packages of peanuts they give you on a plane? How many in one?"

"How many peanuts? Oh, they're generally broken so it's hard to tell, but I guess there are between twenty and twenty-five."

"Twenty-two."

"Is that a fact?" Her voice began to tremble. In an effort to calm herself, Cheryl glanced at her watch. It was nearly nine—time for visitors to leave.

"I have to go, Richard." He was staring at the window and paid no attention. He was like all other men—got the information he wanted and then ignored her. She edged toward the door. "Good night."

"Help me, help me," he chanted, then in a softer voice added: "For God's sake, help me, Cheryl."

Cheryl's eyes began to tear, and she grabbed the metal doorframe for support. "I'll try, Richard. I'll try."

On the way to the car she berated herself for being so moved by the sound of her own name. After all, Cheryl was considerably easier to say than MacLogan.

Chapter Four

He dipped his comb into the sink, shook it, then parted his hair. Vernice was waiting to shave him. Even though his gold razor had been recovered, Vernice still preferred using a plastic, disposable one. She believed it gave a closer shave. Nurse's aides were supposed to be trained in shaving patients. Vernice probably felt shaving her legs once a week made her an expert and did not attend those classes.

Richard gestured for his razor and the cartridge of Trac II blades, then set the plastic cartridge on his right thigh. As he brought the blade toward the cartridge, it slid into the valley of his lap. The third time this happened, he grabbed the cartridge before Vernice could. At first he intended to hurl it against the wall but instead he just held onto it and let the sharp edges of the plastic dig into his fingers. Then he set it back in his lap and, using his left index finger as a lever, threaded the blade onto its track.

"Very good," Vernice cooed. "Reflexes are improving. We should have gotten you a girlfriend a long time ago."

She used the word *girlfriend* jokingly, like a game show host. In fact, he did have a woman friend. At first he had not been certain. But last night he had tested her again and now he was positive. As the redhead was leaving, she said, "Good night, Richard." He said nothing, so she repeated herself. When he still said nothing, she pouted, stamped one of her short, wide feet and exclaimed, "Damn you."

To soothe her, he merely uttered her name. He pronounced *Cheryl* slowly, carefully, as if he had a pat of melting butter on his tongue. But it was this ability to wound that heartened him. Not that he was a sadist or anything, but right now if he said *fuck you* to Vernice, she would pleasantly reply *you, too* and go on cleaning his razor. Her calm negated his very existence.

However, even she noticed his lighter mood. Generally she wheeled him down the hall and left him in an isolated spot by the window. But today she let his chair face the couch where two elderly residents were talking. "Hi," he said. Neither the old man nor the old woman responded.

He knew the woman. She wore wire-rimmed glasses, resembled a frightened field mouse, and lived across the hall from him. Every weekend a woman, probably her sister, would come and scream at her. "Jesus Christ, Francine. Can't you pick up your underwear? It's a disgrace in here. You should be ashamed. You were brought up better."

Francine would whimper and say, "I think they're stealing my jewelry."

"No one," her sister always replied, "would want your jewelry." The two had probably never gotten on.

The gentleman sitting beside her was bald but well dressed in vest, slacks, and recently polished cordovans. Richard stared down at his own legs. The left one was slack, swollen, and shaded pink and purple toward the ankle. The right still bulged with muscles. Richard tugged the bedgown down, pulled his terrycloth robe around him, then set the left hand in his lap. Often at night he would wake unable to find his left arm. "Arm is gone," he would holler. "Leg is frozen," he would scream. But this was the first time he had surveyed himself in daylight and acknowledged what a wreck he had become.

Francine, the field mouse, touched her hand to her fresh permanent. "Beautician downstairs is no good," she said.

"Looks pretty."

She blushed. It was not rouge. She actually blushed. "Thank you," she said.

Along with his improving vision, maybe he was regaining his touch with the women. Francine displayed fingernails painted a hideous shade of pink. "Maria polished them."

"Real sexy," Richard told her, then wondered if he was laying it on too thick.

The old man looked skeptical, but did not contradict him. "Moving to my son's pretty soon," he murmured.

Richard nodded. "I'm getting married." He shocked himself with that statement. But still it sounded like a good idea. Besides, announcing events in advance often guaranteed their occurrence.

To be honest Cheryl was not the woman of his dreams. Had he to do it over again, he would have married Janey Birch, his high-school sweetheart. She had had long skinny braids, never kept track of his yardage, and taught him how to bake a two-egg cake. But they had both been scared, beaten into submission by the dire forebodings of parents and school assembly sex-education movies like *Wasted Lives* and *The Birth of Twins*. And he always had the premonition that something better was waiting up the road. He used to accompany his mother to St. Ann's Church, look at the trumpeting, pink-tunic-clad angels over the altar, and see not angels but the Iowa Hawkeyes' cheering squad bugling him a welcome. By his junior year of college, he had come to his senses, but Janey was already married to the assistant branch manager at the Lake Worth Savings & Loan.

MacLogan Ross was another story. Incompatibility marred too many facets of their relationship. If he opened a window, she would sneeze; so there had never been much promise of anything permanent between them.

He had no romantic illusions about Cheryl either. She was a recognizable type. The little fat girl who had dieted herself into a dumpy adult. He had seen anxious women like Cheryl, sitting rigidly behind their steering wheels. While driving they would bob their heads up and down like feeding birds to ease their stiffened neck muscles. But if it was possible to will oneself into loving someone, he was going to love Cheryl. He was a twenty-nine-year-old wreck of a man and knew nothing better was waiting down the road. She was his only chance of escaping from here. And it would not be a relationship without reciprocity. Hell, no. He had never been a free-loader, and though he had few remaining physical or financial assets he would, at least, say the right things to her. He knew by her reluctance in removing her belted camel hair coat that she did not much like her shape. So when she complained about her thickness, he would tell her she possessed an amazing abundance of femininity. Though writing poetry had always seemed a sissy occupation, he now knew that if she required it, he could write the stuff.

Richard redirected his attention to the woman on the couch. Generally Francine needed assistance in standing. So Maria would come, place one white-panted knee between the woman's legs, then boost her up by the armpits. But today by pressing with both hands against the wooden arm of the couch, Francine managed to get herself in an erect position and totter toward him. He felt her grab onto then push the handlebars of his chair.

The old man with whom Richard had felt some kinship proved to be no friend. He lifted both the brakes off Richard's chair so Francine was able to push his bare legs against the scratchy wool of the couch. Then with a jolting, jerking motion she turned the chair around and began pushing him toward the hall. He was certain when they passed the information desk that Vernice or some other person in authority would stop them, but no one did. Richard could hear the woman wheeze as she wheeled him. Apparently she had emphysema. At first he felt like Alice falling down the rabbit hole, but he became calmer as they approached his room.

However, instead of taking him into it, Francine pushed the chair in a wide looping arc and forced him into her room. The sister was right. There was underwear on the floor. Richard stared at one of the elasticized front-seamed garments and felt lucky to have been born in the era of control-top panty hose and front-hook bras. Removing a woman from one of these waist-cinching garments must have been a real test of manhood. No wonder males of that era had died young.

Francine picked a long vinyl jewel box off her dresser, then sat on the bed with it. She began dumping jewelry in his lap: a long string of red plastic beads, an ornately jeweled spoon and knife pin set, an enormous flesh-colored brooch. The sister was right again. Nobody would want this stuff. Next Francine pulled out an assortment of rings. She was breathing more regularly now. The wheezing had stopped. "You need," she said, "a ring for your wife."

That was a fact. But these massive dinner rings she was producing were all wrong. Cheryl was already thoroughly weighted to earth. She needed jewelry that was dainty and light. Out of the rhinestone creations on his lap, he picked up a small red stone in a gold setting, guarded by two tiny diamond chips.

"Garnet," Francine told him with no particular appreciation. "Take it. I have no use for it." He was tempted to accept her offer, but what if later she accused him of thievery. Then he realized there was little chance of that. He could not navigate his own chair. Even if she accused him, no one would believe it. The bedgowned bandit—it would be a joke to the staff. He was a threat to no one.

He jammed the ring on the tip of his left pinkie. "Thank you. Thank you very much." He was not sure what to call her. Using her first name sounded presumptuous.

It did not matter. She had her back to him and was staring into her closet; maybe she was picking out a dress for his wedding. Richard supposed since she had supplied the engagement ring he and Cheryl would have to invite her.

He remained still as a stone, waiting for her to wheel him back to the lobby. He glanced at her window. It was paneless and uninteresting. Besides, for the last couple of days he had abandoned his preoccupation with windowpanes and numbers. His brain was acting like Heinz let off the leash—running full tilt with all sorts of unrelated observations passing through. Right now he was thinking about God—that the Almighty had to be like a player in a Monopoly game. When one of His pieces got a *go to jail* card, he would grieve but be powerless to change the situation.

Richard waited a few more minutes, then craned his neck to see if Francine was still at the closet. She was not. All he could see of her bed was a bit of fringed black afghan, but he could hear breathing. Soft and rhythmic. She must have lain on her bed and fallen asleep. So much for his chauffeur. He lifted his foot pedal and with much toe action and several collisions managed to maneuver his chair into the corridor. The last physical therapist had told him to lead with his good knee. But the motion kept plunging him into the hall wall.

Finally Vernice spotted and rescued him. ''Sugar! We been looking for you. It's time for lunch.'' She wheeled him into his room, then pushed his chair over the bar in his bedside table. Besides confining him, such positioning made him feel like a diner on an airplane. (He disliked airplane food and was always amazed at his teammates, who could ingest enormous quantities of the unidentifiable dinner.)

Vernice uncapped his plate. Fish—greasy vile-smelling flounder. ''I don't want it, Vernice. Take it away, please.'' The fumes from the fish caused his stomach to heave upward like a Frisbee thrown skyward. "Please take it away, Vernice."

"Try a little bit," she answered, and left.

Hot tears, unwilled as a sneeze, rolled down his cheeks. The tears angered him more than the unwanted fish. With a gentle flick of the wrist he pushed the tray off the table and watched it fall. The cup slid off the saucer, rolled to the far wall, then broke. His action, he knew, would not endear him to the staff, but what difference did it make? He was getting married and moving out soon anyway.

Richard stared at the window, endowing each pane with a word, instead of a number: *An amateur Christian, altered by circumstance, with unbendable knees* . . . Doubting his poetic prowess, he switched to the traditional *Our Father*. He had not completely accepted his own theory of an unobtrusive God and still thought God the Father, the Field General, could occasionally intercede in an emergency. Richard was now praying that the circumstances involving himself and the redhead would improve.

Chapter Five

S he felt like the child at the dinner table, a difficult child at that. One who at any moment might blurt out a statement both distressing and embarrassing. Cheryl knew she should not feel that way. She was in her own home at her own table and was serving an appetizing Easter dinner to her mother and stepfather.

And Al, as usual, was eating and drinking daintily—a sliver of ham, a spoonful of salad, a splash of wine. That was what infuriated her so—his damned daintiness. The man's neck was nearly as thick as her mother's waist. The cords in his arms bulged like mature carrots. Just to maintain his frame, he must eat like a horse, and yet at her home he picked. He was dressed casually in a short-sleeved, red knit shirt and slacks of shiny blue material. He must not have gone to Easter services. Cheryl supposed she should not be so judgmental about that since she had not been to Mass herself. But she knew her mother had. Rose, dressed in a beige suit and brown silky blouse that harmonized nicely with her short dark hair, was more angularly attractive than pretty, but she had absolutely beautiful feet. They were long, fine-boned, and perfectly shaped to fill the expensive, narrow Italian shoes she always wore. Today the shoes were two-toned—chocolate-colored on one side and creamy beige on the other—with slender straps around the side and back. But Cheryl could no longer admire them since they were completely hidden under the massive pine dining table.

36

"We are having," Rose was saying, "different people come in at school and speak on their careers. Mostly civil service employees, because they get time off from work. But one of the fathers, an accountant, came in and, Cheryl, I was wondering if you could get away?"

"I kind of doubt Mr. Derrigo or Raymond would go for it." She might have been able to take an early lunch, but Cheryl had no desire to speak to children about secretarial careers. Her mother would not understand. Rose in her own small world was an authority figure, whereas a seasoned secretary whose bosses have not yet arrived for the day, when questioned "Nobody in yet?" will say "That's right," barely conscious of the slight. It was not a career about which she wanted to proselytize to school-children. But to admit such feelings would wound her mother, so she quietly got up for the key lime pie. In deference to Al, she did not say "Dad's favorite."

Rose knew anyway. On this as on all holidays, Cheryl was very conscious of her father's absence. George Farrell would have bought them both orchids. He also would have been wearing his three-piece suit. George Farrell always wore a suit coat and vest, had even died in one, four years before on a train bound for New York. His death had delayed the commuters on the New Haven line a full half hour; it was the first time her father, a charmingly shy, overweight man, had ever inconvenienced anyone.

When she set the pie on the table, Rose shook her head emphatically. "None for me, dear. We have to go eat pasta at Al's mother's house yet."

So that was it! They were eating so sparingly because they were bound for an Italian feast. Cheryl carefully carried the rejected pie out to the kitchen, then filled three large coffee mugs exactly three-quarters full, hoping precision would prevent her from exhibiting her hurt feelings. But when she brought in the coffee, Al, who found sweets sickening, said, "If you're still offering that pie, I'll have a piece."

"You don't need to."

"Looked real good." She might have believed him, except that he ate the lime pudding and baked meringue morosely, making small sniffing noises as if performing some sort of public penance. Then he wiped his mouth and said, "Why don't you come to Mom's with us? She always makes about fifty times too much."

Cheryl hesitated. Just as she was about to say okay, her mom shot Al a look of extreme gratitude, and she knew she was not part of this family and never would be. It was so unfair. Al had a mother of his own; why did he need hers?

"Thanks, but I have plans."

"What plans, hon?"

She sometimes thought her mother had an aversion to using her first name. The name had obviously been her father's choice. Her mother was too sensible to have named a child Cheryl Farrell.

Cheryl hesitated. She had not expected to be questioned and had no ready reply, but then she thought of Richard Olsen. "I visit a stroke patient at the nursing home."

That was only partially true; because Vernice, who had suggested she come, now suggested she not come. "He's getting too attached and calling you his girlfriend." Though the harm in that had not been apparent to Cheryl, she had forced herself to do the right thing and had stopped going. Now she wished she could quit letting people bully her so. She had allowed her mother to talk her into accepting this condo when she would have been far better off, socially if not financially, remaining in her efficiency apartment, surrounded by other singles. And she had allowed Vernice to prevent her from seeing Richard, who wasn't so appalling to talk to. He generally listened, depending on the degree of his own physical discomfort, which was about as much as you could ask of anyone.

Rose looked surprised but satisfied with Cheryl's excuse. "That's lovely of you, dear."

When they had gone, Cheryl took the lily her mom had bought out to the car. At 2:15 she signed in at the main desk of the Michael Keep Home. Though it was a holiday, only two visitors' names preceded hers. On her way upstairs in the chilly elevator Cheryl realized she had come close to losing the perfect friend, one who was always available. She passed the third-floor nurses' station quickly and with head down, just in case Vernice was watching.

Though Cheryl could not keep herself from peeking into patients' rooms, she tried not to dwell on what she saw. To fully acknowledge the white-haired, moaning woman or the old man exposing a gray, limp penis was to admit life was an uncontrollable mess. She began to hurry down the corridor. Her vinyl-soled shoes made sighing, squishing noises as they hit the green tiles. She wondered how Richard existed day after day in this depressing place. Perhaps he had been waiting these last two weeks for the sound of her feet. The thought made her flush and walk even faster.

She made an abrupt right turn into his room. "Richard," she said before noticing that the bed was empty. Not just empty but completely made and covered with a plain white spread. The room had a sterile, unoccupied look. Even Richard's plastic garbage can had no liner. Cheryl was afraid to set down the lily. The room seemed so funereal. What if . . . ? She walked slowly back to the nurses' station and whispered "Richard Olsen?" to the volunteer on duty.

"In the lobby."

Cheryl's eyes followed the woman's finger. Though she was relieved Richard was still alive, seeing him sitting up was a terrible shock. He had his back to her and was leaning forward in his wheelchair, like one of those plastic toy birds that bends down and drinks water from a glass. A white sheet was tied around his middle to secure

him in place. When she approached from the side, she
could see his eyes were vacant, his mouth hung open,
and he was drooling. Something terrible had happened
to him since she had last been there. Always before he
had been unseeing and stubborn, but had never worn this
slobbering, lobotomized look. The only explanation was
that he had suffered another stroke.

Cheryl set the plant on the floor beside his chair and
began rubbing his cold, bent left hand. "Aw, Richard,
aw, Richard," she said softly as tears began rolling down
her cheeks. She watched his yellow slipper as it rhythmically tapped against the floor. Then the floor motion
became more agitated. When she looked up, Richard was
crying, too. On her first visit his tears had terrified her.
But now she was enormously relieved by them. His mouth
had straightened, his eyes had focused and he was trying
to say something. "I, ah, uh. I, ah."

Cheryl noticed there was a picture window in front of
them and a half circle of old people in wheelchairs, staring not out the window but at them. She stood, hiked up
the elasticized waistband on her dirndl skirt, then pushed
at his chair, intending to take him someplace private.
When the chair did not budge, she knelt down again,
embarrassed that she cared what these old people were
thinking. Both Stu and Al considered her childish and
superficial. Maybe they were right.

Richard took one last jagged sigh, shook his head savagely, then said, "I prayed you were safe and coming
soon." He shook his head again. "You didn't come."

His intense reaction to her absence required a lie. "I
was sick. But I'm okay now."

Richard straightened his back, then leaned down and
pulled toward him a gray plastic-coated lever on the right
side of the chair. He gestured for her to remove the brake
on the left side. Then he commanded, "Take me to my
room, Cheryl."

The dramatic change in him amused her. "Yes, boss."
She placed the plant in his lap, and he grasped it with

his good arm. This time the chair moved easily. Richard was wearing a pale blue bedgown with a gaping neckline that revealed the freckles on his back. As soon as they were in his room, she took the plant, moved the restricting sheet, pulled a robe from the closet, and draped it around his shoulders. "Better, Richard?"

"Mmm," he mumbled with little conviction. Then he pulled something off his left finger and thrust it at her. Before she could grasp it, the small object fell from his hand and rolled toward the wall. Halfway to his window, she found a small gold ring. "Where did this come from?"

"They tried to take it from me. I thought it was them that wouldn't let you come anymore."

He was smiling tightly, close to tears again. Cheryl calmly repeated, "Where did it come from?"

"The old woman. We'll have to invite her."

She had no idea what he was talking about but was reluctant to question him. All that mattered was that he had missed her.

"Okay." Cheryl slipped the ring on her right hand.

"Other hand."

Feeling reprimanded, she handed the ring back to Richard, who carefully threaded it on her left finger. "I think we should kiss now," he said in the same tone her mother had once used to say "I think you should shake hands now" when introducing her to a blind child.

They kissed solemnly and Cheryl knew she was committing a rash, impetuous act. But this was the way it always happened in the novels.

Chapter Six

At first Richard thought the man was a musician. The curly hair was deceptive. And his speech was slow and metered. His fingers, with their well-manicured nails, held an expensive silver pen. There was a spiral binder open on his lap.

"Richard, could you name the first president of the United States?"

"George Washington."

"Can you name any of the signers of the Declaration of Independence?"

Richard had almost decided the guy with the curls was a history major turned reporter when he asked, "Since the onset of your illness, has any of your family been to visit you?"

"My mom came once."

"Just once?"

"She doesn't like being around sick people."

"And how does that make you feel?"

That's when he knew his companion was some sort of psychiatrist. Richard shrugged and looked at his window longingly. He could start counting in increments of something easy like fifteens and tune this guy right out.

"Do you have any other visitors?"

Richard redirected his attention to his visitor. This shrink was administering some sort of test, and until he knew its purpose and consequences he had better keep alert.

"A woman named Cheryl comes."

"Your fiancée?"

"Yeah."

"And what do you expect of this upcoming marriage?"

"To care about somebody. To have somebody care about me."

"Do you expect it to restore your health?"

Before he could give the correct, the reasonable answer, the orderly came in, put a hand behind his sweating back, and swung him into a sitting position. Visitor or no, it was ten o'clock in the morning and time for him to get up. The nursing-home schedule never varied, except today Vernice had skipped his bath, and he missed that. The ministrations of a warm, wet rag limbered his legs immensely. Now he was dizzy and his legs felt like breaking Popsicle sticks. The orderly steadied him on the edge of the bed while Richard stared down at his own bare feet. "Need my slippers," he told the Indian. But the orderly paid no attention and in his hurry to depart he slammed him into the wheelchair like a billiard ball sunk into the pocket. He left without ever speaking.

The psychiatrist had absorbed the whole humiliating transaction, and Richard knew it was now no use. Even giving the right answers would not make him appear less pathetic. He devoted his attention to the window: 15–30–45–60–75–90–105.

Suddenly he felt his right foot being lifted. It was no muscle spasm; the doctor was down on both knees, pulling on his elasticized yellow slippers. This unsolicited kindness unnerved Richard, made his insides feel as chaotic and jumbled as a popcorn popper. Besides the orderly, no man had touched him since his stroke. No man had even looked him full in the face. Even Jetlag, his best friend, stood at the end of his hospital bed those first few days mumbling, "You need anything, Buddy?"—and carefully avoiding eye contact.

He had wanted to scream, "Hold me, help me!" But

Jetlag, uncomfortable as a caged dog, had wanted to bolt, so Richard had let him go. He had let them all go.

With long sure strokes, the psychiatrist rubbed the blackness out of the left leg, then covered Richard's lap with the terrycloth robe. "Is there someplace private we could go, where there's an ashtray?" he asked. "I'd like a cigarette."

He knew the guy was a professional who could go for long periods of time without a cigarette. This head doctor was playing some devious game. Willing to play along, Richard pointed down the hall.

As the doctor began pushing his chair, it occurred to Richard he had become a lot like Heinz at the pound—completely unselective and more than willing to go off with anyone who was kind to him.

Halfway down the hall the doctor asked, "Do you worry about having another episode?" Then quickly added: "You shouldn't, you know. It's very unlikely."

Episode? Must be another term for it. And he thought he had heard them all: shock, thrombosis, aneurysm, hemorrhage, stroke. When the medical experts couldn't find a cure, they compensated with synonyms. ("No. Lightning never strikes the same tree twice.")

Once they were inside the visitors' lounge, the doctor closed the door with an emphatic slam. Richard appreciated that. Spared Vernice's relentless scrutiny, he was even prepared for the obligatory question about football.

"You watch much sports?"

"No." When he was first hospitalized, the nurses kept his TV tuned to ESPN and Sports Channel. But his vision had still been blurred then, and all those athletic endeavors were about as interesting as studying an anthill. So he had taken the TV wand and flipped from station to station, until his roommate complained and the remote-control device was taken from him.

With a rolling motion the curly-headed doctor pushed the sand-filled, circular-based ashtray over by the window and began exhaling little smoke rings. As they got

larger Richard wondered if this was some type of exam
where he would be asked what objects the smoke rings
most resembled. At first, he thought, they looked like
LifeSavers but they began to remind him of little sugar
doughnuts (the kind that come twenty-four to a package).
It didn't matter, for the psychiatrist's next question had
nothing to do with smoke rings.

"Do you have any long-term goals, Richard?" Silence. The doctor rephrased the question. "If you marry,
how will that change your life?"

"I'll try and make the woman happy."

"That's admirable, but does your fiancée have any
traits you don't like?"

Richard grimaced. He was not going to get caught bad-
mouthing his intended. You take what you're given and
make the best of it. That was his philosophy. He had
always been loyal to his offensive linemen. For every time
they'd left him vulnerable, he could remember the hundred times they'd plowed down the opposition.

For some reason his nonanswer upset the man. The
guy half cringed and said, "This is awkward for us, isn't
it? I guess you know I was briefly married to Cheryl, and
it's hard for me to assess your competency for something
I was not successful at."

The husband! This was her husband? She still used his
name, too. But he couldn't remember it. God Almighty!
He was going to marry the woman, and he couldn't remember her last name. H-a-s-k-e-l-l? No, Haskell had
been an English prof back in Iowa. He watched as the
psychiatrist ground out his third cigarette and began to
pace back and forth on the white tile floor. Richard was
amazed. He could not remember names, could not
frighten Vernice with his worst curses, but he had somehow managed to put this overeducated appraiser on the
defensive.

"The whole fiasco was my fault," the man stated.
"Coming down the aisle, I knew it was a mistake. It was
like taking on a full-time patient instead of a wife. Cheryl's

looking for another father. She doesn't know what she wants.''

Richard did not find that such an unalterable shortcoming. It was simply a matter of telling her what to do. But he nodded sympathetically, while the doctor continued pacing. This transition from patient to person with opinions bewildered him. The high-school quarterbacks' manual stated, ''Luck is preparation meeting opportunity.'' He had believed that until Easter Sunday when the woman came back. She had stopped visiting for no good reason and had started again the same way. Now he knew that luck was just luck. A bit of hymn began to tease him. ''I was lost but now am . . .'' ''I was lost but now am . . .'' *Saved? Freed? Found?* And then he remembered his fiancée's name was Cheryl Freedman.

''That's not to say she's not a good woman. A shapely one, too.'' Freedman gave him a conspiratorial grin.

Richard wondered if the psychiatrist/ex-husband's whole performance wasn't a sly way of testing his sexual appetites. Just in case he nodded appreciatively—though all he had noticed about Cheryl's shape was that she was ashamed of it. And he had no appetites. Food did not interest him. At dinnertime he would tear the plastic wrapper from the bread and eat the single white slice, but nothing else. Sex was no different. It was women who had betrayed him. How could he be attracted to them? Though from the first he had known Cheryl was too meek and self-doubting to be part of that conspiracy. ''Cheryl is not like other women.''

For some reason that remark silenced Freedman and ended the interview. The psychiatrist wheeled Richard back to his room, shook his hand, wished him luck, and left.

Richard remained with his back to the door, his bladder about to burst, and the belt to his bathrobe caught in the spokes of his right wheel. He could see the plastic urinal on his bedside table but could make no progress toward it. When he heard two pairs of feet advancing into his room, he urgently called, "Urinal, Vernice. Please."

There was a cessation of sound and movement and then a man's deep voice replied, "Okay." A woman's voice added: "I'll wait in the hall."

The man apparently thought Richard needed to stand up. After getting him the urinal, he pushed him into the bathroom, grabbed him under the armpits, and raised him onto his feet. The altitude or something made Richard feel acutely ill. "Can do it sitting?" The man eased him back into the chair.

When the urinal was emptied, the stranger washed his hands thoroughly, then picked the white washcloth off the rack and scrubbed Richard's hand and entire upper right arm. Though he was large and muscled like the orderly, he was dressed in civilian clothes, and Richard did not know if he was staff or not. Frankly he was too tired and dizzy to care.

The man dried Richard's diminished throwing arm and said, "Back three years ago me and my buddies flew down to Florida and saw you beat Miami in Miami. Won three hundred dollars on that game. Paid for my whole trip."

Richard restlessly tapped his foot against the floor. "Help me into bed."

"Oh, sure."

His bed was his home, his refuge, and the chemically treated sheets felt like cold silk against the backs of his bare legs. Now safely in bed, he could smell the musky cologne of the man who had helped him. Though he generally distrusted scented men, this guy did not seem like a bad sort. Richard yawned and his useless left arm jerked reflexively.

"Got to get Rose, my wife," the man said. "She's real anxious to meet you."

Richard nodded amiably and closed his eyes. In a few seconds he heard the purposeful clicks of a woman's heels. Without opening his eyes he knew Rose was tall.

"He fell asleep," the man pronounced just as Richard was about to open his eyes and look at the wife.

"Looks so innocent, doesn't he?" the woman whispered. "At least he won't abuse her or run around on her."

Richard decided his best bet was to fake deep sleep.

"Are you kidding? We can't let her go through with this. She couldn't take care of him. The poor devil is a deadweight lift."

"She didn't stop us. We can't stop her. If she had raised one objection, when we were dating . . . Let's go. Come back later."

The man said nothing. He had probably heard it all before. Richard understood his resigned silence. Women could be very repetitious.

Chapter Seven

That dog, that damn dog, had apparently vanished into thin air. It looked as if it might take a private detective to find him. Cheryl had begun the search at the library by gazing at old newspaper pictures of the sad-eyed mutt, who appeared to be part collie, part German shepherd. The rest of her research was carried out at work in between secretarial duties—which was difficult because both Mr. Raymond and Mr. Derrigo were in.

And Derrigo was helpless. He might fry his own egg at home, but at work he was unwilling to dial even local calls. "Cheryl," he would bellow, "get me Joe Krupa." She would punch the numbers of Software's local sales office, then transfer Mr. Krupa into Derrigo. But now he was roaring "Get me Bill Gamage" just when she had finally gotten someone at the bankrupt Connecticut Clippers' business office to answer the phone. Cheryl held up two restraining fingers. But unwilling to wait, Derrigo placed the call himself. "D-E-R-R-I-G-O," she heard him spell, the irritation of being forced to explain the obvious evident in his voice.

"I'm sorry," the Clippers' bookkeeper came back on, "we have no information on Richard Olsen."

"Okay, thank you."

"Cheryl," Mr. Raymond was calling. His position was slightly inferior to Derrigo's, and his view of the secretary more restricted. He could never tell when she was on the phone. Cheryl rose slowly and walked into his office. It was no use. She could not call around about

49

Richard's dog at work, and at home without the force of an international corporation behind her, she would stutter and stammer. The only alternative was to send letters. Despite extensive research at the library, Cheryl had been able to locate only two of Richard's former teammates. Bob Knesch was with Pittsburgh and Joe "Jetlag" Johnson played for Miami. She sent the men identical requests to write or phone her collect if they knew the whereabouts of Richard's dog. It was the best she could do.

Cheryl was wearing a silky white blouse and black slacks. The wide-sleeved blouse minimized her ample bust, and the dark slacks slimmed and elongated her. She always wore her most flattering outfits when Derrigo was in. It was just habit now, but right after her father died, Derrigo had been the most important man in her life. Not only did he stop at her desk during harassed moments and ask "How's it going, hon?" but he also saved the end of the day for her—those seven minutes between the closing click of his Samsonite briefcase and the departure of his van pool. Some days this exclusive attention still made her feel important, loyal, and loved. But she now knew the man's tactics were no more sincere than Raymond's; he was just a better manager.

"What do they look like?" Richard had asked. She had been unable to explain Derrigo's sad-eyed charm, how powerful and charismatic he looked in his brown suit coats, or how, when he removed them to reveal baggy slacks and a sinking posterior, he resembled agrarian ancestors with hoes more than an executive.

She finally answered lamely, "He wears brown a lot." She had done better by Raymond, describing him as imperial, long-fingered, and gray-complexioned.

Richard had begun to call them Mr. Brown and Mr. Gray. He had a way of focusing on a single physical aspect and naming the person for it. The timid woman across the hall was Mouse. The chubby-cheeked aide was Chipmunk. Cheryl herself he often referred to as The

Woman, as if she somehow embodied all female characteristics. It was even simpler than that. She had become his window, the sole object of his attention. And though this was not the type of romance she read about, she could not go back to the monotony of life without him.

At 4:23 Derrigo appeared at the side of her desk. "Well, we made it through another week."

"Sure did." Cheryl smiled and tossed her hair back. "How's Stu?"

This used to be her favorite time, and the reason she worked so industriously all day. Though never really married, Cheryl had been gratified that a man of Derrigo's importance, whose photo regularly appeared on the cover of *Computer Digest*, took the time to remember Stu's name. But now she blinked and looked at him, about to utter the usual "Oh, fine." But cold, unfamiliar hatred prevented her from speaking. Regardless of his stature, how could Derrigo have lived with her through that awful time and not known she had been rejected and deserted. The bastard! For all his sad-eyed sympathy he knew her no better than her bank teller. She blinked again. "My husband's not doing well. He's been having awful, awful headaches. I'm real worried."

Derrigo nodded with immediate comprehension. "Stress," he said, "all this damn stress." His programmed watch gave its high-pitched 4:30 P.M. bleep—time to meet his van.

Cheryl was glad Derrigo, the Catholic, commuted back to New York State. Her banns were to be announced at St. Peter's, the local Roman Catholic church, that Sunday, and reading them might have confused him. At 4:40 Raymond also left. "Good night, dear."

"Good night, Mr. Raymond."

Richard gauged time by the TV set of the woman across the hall. When the *Mary Tyler Moore* rerun ended, it was time for Cheryl to come. But tonight she was late. The CBS News was on, and Richard was watching the door.

Her heart always beat crazily when he first gave her his easy, sloppy smile. He did not look so different from the newspaper photographs she kept of him. Only in approaching the bed could one see how his left shoulder slumped and how bent his arm was. Cranberry juice or some other pink liquid had been spilled near the collar of his bedgown. "You're late," he said.

Cheryl displayed a white bag. "I brought you french fries." She set them on his nightstand, then sank wearily into the uncomfortable visitor's chair, glad her evenings of sitting in it were coming to an end. "I'm getting Brown and Gray primed, Richard. Next week I'm requesting a leave because my husband is sick."

"Yeah?"

Richard was eating the french fries a little too quickly. What appeared to be ravenous hunger, Cheryl decided, was more a matter of impaired reflexes. He refilled his mouth before it was emptied because his timing was shot. She ripped open one of the white packets of ketchup and said, "Want to dip them in here?" That added business slowed the eating process and kept him from choking. She knew better than to ask him to slow down or issue any commands. If she did, he would just ignore her.

He finished the french fries. "I shouldn't have eaten them," he said.

She looked at his long cadaverous frame. "Why not?"

"Shouldn't have." He was staring at his body with the same disgust with which she viewed her own. It was not the calories he regretted, she realized, but his own persistent clinging to life that shamed and embarrassed him.

She walked over by his bed. "You crazy man. You've got to eat. I need you." She affectionately pushed a thatch of hair off his forehead. His hair was as fine as a baby's, and she touched it often, perhaps because she had so little else to become attached to.

Generally it was a man's car over which she got sen-

timental. Cheryl remembered how she used to feel about
Stuart's orange Karmen Ghia with the little sunroof. Even
before they were dating just a glimpse of his car was
enough to send her reeling. Even after all the disappoint-
ments that followed, the sight of one of those orange
Volkswagens made her heart pound and her palms get
sweaty. It was strange how the distinction between the
man and the car got blurred. Spotting a gray Cadillac
like her father's made her ache all over. Those big cars
looked so safe and important and propelled her back to
the time when she could call her father and the secretary
put her right through. Now she did the same thing for
Derrigo's daughter.

Cheryl wondered what kind of car Richard had driven.
All she knew was that he had signed it over to his mother
shortly after being hospitalized. Stuart told her that. She
had supposed there would be some legal complications
in marrying an institutionalized man, but, according to
Stuart, noncompetency had never been established; so
Richard was free to make his own decisions.

She supposed it was kind of tacky to send Stuart. But
he had said, "If I can ever help . . ." And she knew he
would be professional. Besides, she had wanted him to
challenge her motives. Was she marrying Richard in order to nurse a father who had died too quickly? To prove
her unselfishness to a husband who had never given her
the chance? Et cetera, et cetera. And she wanted an opportunity to defend Richard's mental health, had even
prepared a little speech: "I know the staff thinks he's
cracked, but it's just his way of trying to maintain dignity." She never got a chance to use it. Stuart had been
absolutely awed by Richard's intelligence, his willpower,
and the strength of his feeling for her. That was the trouble with psychiatrists. They never did what you thought
they would. She had believed Stuart with his heightened
sensitivity would make the ideal spouse. She couldn't
have been more wrong.

Richard was restless. He raised himself by pulling on

the metal triangle over his head. Then he slid down a bit;
and by pushing with his good side, managed to grab the
left bed rail. Throughout all this activity he watched her
steadily. "What did Brown say?"

"When I told him my husband was sick? Oh, just a
lot of phony sympathy." The vinyl on the visitor's chair
squawked as she sat down and pushed herself backward.
"My back and neck are killing me. All that type, type,
typing." She ducked her head. "Brown! He's such a
phony. But God, Richard, there was a time when I wanted
to impress him so damn bad. I used to pretend some
derelict broke in and Derr—Brown defended me. But finally I got to pretending a band of terrorists came in and
that I was the one who saved both Brown and Gray."
Richard was gazing at her with such rapt attention, she
thought he must have experienced similar emotions, must
have constructed similar desperate daydreams, hoping to
win a surrogate father or substitute mother. "Guess you
went through the same thing with somebody. Huh?"

He shook his head gravely. "No, never."

She stood and took his left hand. A mosquito had bit-
ten him, and the skin around his large white knuckle
was red and swollen. To Cheryl, the mosquito bite
emphasized how defenseless he was. Her inability to
protect him made her feel even more exhausted. "Richard, I've got to go home. Good night." It was a cold
exit, she reckoned, but she never called him sugar,
sweetie, or such endearments because the staff used them
so effusively.

Cheryl went home to her book. At work she was still
reading the Regencies, but in bed at night she had grav-
itated toward medical tomes about cardiovascular disease.
It disconcerted her that she always read the paragraph
about resuming sexual activity before reading the chap-
ters on therapy and depression. The paragraphs were
never conclusive: some could; some could not. The books
were helpful in other ways, though. Studying the analyses
of prestroke symptoms, combined with what Richard had

told her, increased her confidence for the performance that lay ahead.

"How's Stu?" Derrigo asked again.

"Still having the headaches and acting funny. Wants to go on vacation. Doesn't want to go on vacation. Feels dizzy a lot."

A week later it was Raymond she told first—mainly because he arrived at the office before Derrigo. Her eyes, after a night of poor sleep, were in a state appropriate for delivering tragic information. "My husband's had a stroke. I'm going to have to request a leave of absence."

Raymond set down his cigar, then looked at her for a moment without comprehending. He stared at her empty hands as if they might provide some clue to this interruption of the morning routine. Finally he said, "Of course. Whatever you need."

When Derrigo heard the news, he offered to drive her home. "Oh, no," she told him bravely. "He's in the hospital and being well cared for."

Later that afternoon Derrigo heard her on the phone ordering a hospital bed. Both he and Raymond were deferential. They tightened up their prose to keep letters and memos brief and they put callers on hold in order to pull out a file for themselves. Cheryl reviewed these developments with a degree of amusement; it seemed a shame to start her leave just as the office was turning civilized.

On Wednesday an office temporary, who was to fill in for her, arrived. The agency had said the woman's name was Lucy. Cheryl approached the reception desk expecting to meet a middle-aged woman. But Lucy was young—very young. She wore high-waisted black slacks and a tight pink knit top pulled over a firm chest. As they walked back to Cheryl's desk Lucy's high-heeled sandals made a slap, slop, slap, slop sound. Cheryl noticed that Lucy's toes were painted the same shade of pink as her top. She felt the beginnings of a headache but carefully explained her responsibilities and showed Lucy the phone and files. Lucy smiled constantly and asked only one question: ''Where's the ladies' room?''

When Cheryl made introductions to her coworkers, Lucy said hello sweetly but almost inaudibly. As they were leaving Derrigo's office she batted her artificial eyelashes and asked, ''Would you like coffee or anything?''

With no little trouble Cheryl had cured Derrigo of his dependence on her for coffee. The task had been all the more difficult because the woman who had preceded her had been the motherly type eager to perform such personal services. And here was this office temporary wrecking it all. She would get their coffee, bring their lunch, type sloppily, scramble phone messages, and they would love her, absolutely love her. Fortunately Derrigo was on his way to a meeting, so he declined Lucy's chirpy offer of coffee. *This time*, Cheryl reflected.

Whir, whir. The child was stuffing pencils into the electric sharpener. She had found something she liked to do. ''Lucy, would you like coffee?''

''No, thank you. I don't drink it.''

Cheryl pulled her large leather purse out of the bottom desk drawer. Lucy's tiny vinyl disco bag was wedged in front of it. What a waste, Cheryl thought. For all these years, she had bought professional-looking, well-tailored clothes when she could have shopped at discount stores like Lucy and been equally appreciated. But that was not really true. Her pear-shaped frame required expensive clothes. It was all so unfair.

Lucy answered the phone and scribbled a message on the green memo pad with her own purple felt-tip pen. Then in fine secretarial style she repeated all the information to the caller. When Lucy gave Derrigo the green slip of paper, he said ''Thank you, hon,'' an endearment Cheryl once thought she had earned by years of devoted service. Cheryl's own phone started ringing, but before she could answer Lucy picked it up. ''Mrs. Freedman's line. Yes, she is. She's right here. May I ask who's calling?''

Lucy finally handed her the phone with an eager-to-please smile. ''It's a Mr. Johnson.''

''Thank you, Lucy.''

''Cheryl?'' asked an unfamiliar voice.

''Speaking.''

''This is Jetlag Johnson. I've got the dog.''

''Pardon me?''

''Heinz. Richard's dog.''

''Oh, well, good.''

''The kids will miss him, but if Richard wants him, I'll put him on a plane.''

It was inconceivable to Cheryl that a man named Jetlag had children.

''But I've got just one question. What's your relationship to Richard?''

''Wife.''

''Recent development?''

''Very. Starts this Sunday.''

''You sure you know what you're getting into?''

A tiny sigh escaped from her. How perceptive of Jetlag Johnson! She had only seen Richard sitting up once. He had been in his wheelchair with a sheet tied around his waist, looking as disembodied as Dan Rather on the seven o'clock news. Besides not knowing Richard that well, she also knew very little about his illness. All her medical reading had not prepared her for that terrifying time when she approached his bed and he looked at her with hard, flat eyes and demanded, ''Take me back to bed.''

''You are in bed, Richard.''

''No, I'm not. Take me back.'' She had known better than to summon help from the nurses or aides. They could not deal with symptoms that were neither overt nor measurable. So she had slowly walked down the hall, and when she returned, Richard was blinking and all right. Was it occasions like this that had driven away all his friends? Or had he been violent, too? Right now she could not ask Jetlag because Lucy was poised over the pencil sharpener waiting for her to finish her conversation. "We'll be all right."

"Well, I'm glad he found you," Jetlag concluded. "Consider Heinz our wedding present."

Wedding present! It sounded so strange, Cheryl thought, as she put the phone back on the hook. She had been so busy before her last wedding—with presents, photographers, florists, the catering service. Perhaps society insisted on this overpreparation so the participants would be too tired, dazed, and dizzy to know what they were doing.

The arrangements for this ceremony had been few. The event would take place in the nursing home chapel. There would be no honeymoon. She had ordered a hospital bed at $118 a month. Home health aides were available from an agency for ten dollars an hour. Since she made only $8.25, they would be dipping into her savings and inheritance right from the start. But she had really expected more obstacles.

Her mother must have read about the banns in her church bulletin, but she had not mentioned it. Cheryl did not know why she was surprised. Her mother never interfered. For months after Cheryl had dropped out of college, she had followed her mother from room to room asking, "Are you upset?" Rose steadfastly refused to betray any emotion. "You are an adult. It is your decision." Actually that was one of the few decisions in her life she did not regret. It had given her two more years to be near her father.

Stuart, the one person she had told about this marriage, had been totally unfatherly. He had called her and babbled on about supremacy and magic of love without ever finding out if Richard could express that love. There were a few days a month when that did matter to her. Stuart had been no help.

Neither had the Catholic Church. The Church placed obstacles in everyone's path but hers. She was a woman whose first marriage had been annulled. Richard's sexual competency was in question. But the young Italian priest who would marry them asked no unpleasant questions and made everything as convenient as possible.

Cheryl moved the freshly sharpened gray pencils from one side of her desk to the other. Somebody should be putting a stop to this marriage. She was a woman who could not take care of an African violet. (The leaves always got jaundiced-looking and she had to rely on her mother's plant-resuscitation powers.) Cheryl moved the pencils back again. But the thing was: somebody ought to love Richard. And somebody also ought to love her. It was too late to change anything anyway. As soon as she had accepted the ring, it had all become as irreversible as a mailed parcel.

Lucy's doe eyes were fixed on Cheryl as she sat there, unmoving, purse in lap. "Would you like me to get the coffee, Mrs. Freedman?"

"That'd be really nice." Cheryl opened her wallet but found nothing but copper. She should be organized like her mother and occasionally roll her pennies. She pulled out a bill but Lucy shook her head and reached for the disco bag. Her gold leaf earrings swayed as she bent down. "I want to get them. You've been so nice and all."

Cheryl sat back, waited, and began to understand men a little better. It was very pleasant to have an attractive, ungrudging young person fetch the coffee.

Chapter Eight

The ring was under his right leg. The ring was under his right leg. He had to remember that. He hoped he would. There was this whole Mass to sit through first, and when the time came he might not remember.

He did not remember much anymore. All week long the Mouse had been asking him what color dress Cheryl would be wearing. He never remembered to ask her. Finally Mouse said, "Will she be wearing white?" He had told her no and been right. Cheryl was wearing a lime-colored dress. It was pretty enough, but he had seen it before. It hurt him that she had not bought a new dress. But it was her second wedding and he supposed that made a difference.

Her long red hair was shiny. She probably slept on hair rollers every night. Women, he had noticed, who were not beautiful sometimes went in for self-mortification— always washing their hair and starving themselves. MacLogan was beautiful, and she had not gone in for self-mortification. Lord, no! When she was in the mood, she could eat like—stop! *Stop!* What was he doing thinking about another woman on his wedding day? Still he wished Cheryl had wound a ribbon through her hair or stuck some dried flowers in it—anything to denote that today was special.

The one who had gone to some pains was the Mouse. She had worn a white two-piece dress with large gold buttons. Her hair had just been worked on by the beautician and each curl was separate, molded, and distinct

like a small hill or a new grave. She was standing at the
altar to the left of Cheryl. They had let her be a witness,
but she was calling herself a bridesmaid.

Al was standing to the right of Richard. He had not
officially asked Cheryl's stepfather to be a witness or his
best man, but Al had been attending to him all day and
continued to do so. It was Al who had bought him the
clothes he was wearing. The navy slacks and white shirt
were painfully stiff, and the new canvas shoes felt like
weights attached to his feet. It was not the time to be
thinking about his feet. He looked over at Cheryl and
smiled, but she was piously watching the priest.

May the Lord God accept the offering from your hands
For the praise and glory of His name
For our good and that of all His Holy Church

His back ached. His feet hurt. But what was the alternative? If he weren't here in the chapel getting married,
he would be in the upstairs lounge staring out at filthy
Birch Lake. "Lord God have mercy." He must have slid
forward and said it out loud, for Al suddenly grabbed
him under the armpits and boosted him back in the chair.
Cheryl's face turned crimson as she stared at him. He
had shamed the woman and himself. If only Vernice
would come and take him back to bed. He searched the
two rows of spectators but did not see her. She was always snooping around when he did not want her. Why
couldn't she just once be around when he needed her?

The altar cloth had eighteen tassels on his side. He
counted twice to be certain. Then he double-checked with
multiples of six and, sure enough, the total was one hundred and eight. Sixteen subtracted from one hundred and
eight was ninety-two. No, it was not. No, God, no. It
was. It was. He looked up. Cheryl was still staring at
him and mouthing something—four words—"Blah, blah,
blah, blah." She did it again: "Blah, blah, blah, blah."

Then she looked at him inquisitively. "Are you all right?"

He finally figured it out and nodded. "Yes."

It was a stupid question. But at least she was asking. For the last two years people had been constantly telling him he was all right. When his body had first started causing him petty humiliations, he had gone to the team doctor. Eckert told him he was fine, just getting older. He had been twenty-seven years old at the time. Then after he had the stroke, the physical therapists dragged him around while the pain shot up and down. When he screamed, they took his blood pressure and pronounced, "You're all right, Richard. You're all right." He was not all right; but at least the woman asked rather than told.

The priest lifted the host. "This is my body." Richard raised his head then bowed it. Christ had died on the cross and his own body was half-dead. In the land of the living they call it crippled.

The crippled Connecticut Clippers. That's what the new team had been called before he was drafted. He had gone with the hapless Iowa Hawks to the Rose Bowl, and the Connecticut owners had wanted him to turn things around for them. Even if he had stayed in good health, he never could have. He had been a worthy player—conscientious, consistent, and sufficiently strong-willed—but never capable of magic. Tony Travano, the high-school quarterback he had followed at Flagler High, had been capable of it. The guy would stare at himself with loathing in the lavatory mirror before games quietly muttering, "Wop, greaser. You stink! You suck!" Occasionally he could work himself up into an emotional frenzy sufficient to go out and perform the impossible. But Travano had lasted only one year in the pros. The fans, the press, had wanted his magic to be consistent. They did not understand that you had to choose.

The press had been kinder to Richard, constantly labeling him amiable, though he was not all that amiable.

He just possessed a slightly protruding arc of upper teeth that made him look as if he were always smiling.

When he was a kid, there had been no money for orthodontia. His father, a minor-league ballplayer, had deserted his mother when Richard was three years old. He did not remember his father, only the portable ironing board his mother had used during their vagabond time as a family. His mother was rightfully bitter, and Richard knew he had to excel at football and make it up to her. But with his sickness he had broken the deal. And now he was becoming a man just like his father—a man who lived off women.

He looked over at Cheryl, and there she was dazed and walking toward him. The overhead lights bounced eerily off her red hair. She passed right in front of the altar without stopping to genuflect or anything. You weren't supposed to do that. Was she nuts? She must have decided she could not go through with it and was stopping the ceremony. He could understand. Ten minutes earlier he had wanted to do the same thing himself. When Cheryl got right in front of him, she extended her freckled hand and said "Peace of Christ be with you."

The kiss of peace! He tugged at her upper arm. Apparently thinking he wanted more than a handshake, she bent down and brushed her lips against his hairline. "Genuflect on your way back," he whispered.

"Ahh." She covered her mouth with her hand in an embarrassed *oops* gesture. But on the way back she respectfully, almost gracefully dipped down in front of the altar. When they were facing each other, she gave him an anxious look.

He smiled approvingly. *You did fine. You are all right.* The woman needed confidence.

Playing football was supposed to give you confidence, and in isolated moments during actual games it did. But between times you were everybody's monkey. You could get cut or traded, and the press badgered you with unanswerable questions.

The one time you did want to speak to the press and explain a questionable action in a complicated play, they dismissed you with a "Know you want to get to the showers, Richard." It was not much different from his relationship with Vernice. Playing football probably prepared you for being a stroke patient as well as any vocation.

And through it all—one good, one fair, and one poor season—he had received the bubble gum. The gift's very constancy moved him. It was so nonjudgmental, he figured it had to be sent by a small child. Every time he spoke at the grade schools on the importance of warming up, he would look for the child, whom he had named Chucky Freedman.

In every auditorium there was always one kid, a little more intense than the others, his very love for the game made all the more poignant by his fragile physique. Richard imagined that this kid played football—all by himself, but he played. He would be the kid alone in the snowy vacant lot with a wool hat pulled down to his cheeks, tiny wrists poking out of a windbreaker with an NFL insignia on it. And he would not even be playing with a real football, just one of those bright blue or orange foam jobs. But he'd spot his imaginary receivers, make the snap, and be playing pure ball, unadulterated by greed, commentators, or prime-time television.

But there had never been a Chucky Freedman. And Cheryl, he was damn sure—would even put money on it—had never thrown a football in her life. So what did it all mean? He didn't know.

Al nudged him. "Ring," he whispered, and began pushing Richard's chair toward the center. The ring, the ring, the ring was where? He panicked for a second, but then the answer came to him with the certainty of a memorized response from the Baltimore Catechism. (Who made you? God made me to show forth his goodness.) The ring was under his right leg. The ring was under his right leg.

His hand was steady as he slipped the ring onto her finger. True to form, she had no ring for him. Just as she had not bought a new dress or put a ribbon in her hair.

After they exchanged vows, he went with Cheryl and her parents to the all-purpose room. Cheryl had been surprised that he knew Rose and Al. But Good Lord!— did she think they would just let her marry anybody?

There was a pile of gifts on a table in there. Cheryl flushed with pleasure. She had not expected gifts, and their quality did nothing to diminish her pleasure. She gushed over each one. First she displayed plastic place mats, which had been made by laminating used birthday and get-well cards in the arts and crafts class. "We'll have to invite you all for dinner and use these," she said, smiling at the Mouse and her girlfriend.

They most certainly would not have these people over, Richard reflected. But maybe Cheryl said things out of nervous politeness. He would have to understand her more fully. His very survival depended on it.

Next she held up a rhinestone-eyed cat made from a light bulb attached to a beer bottle and spray-painted gold. "For my dresser," she cooed. Most of the other items were innocuous and utilitarian: washcloths, pot holders, and dish towels.

When the presents were cleared from the table, Vernice and Maria came in with a massive sheet cake. Cheryl, knife in hand, moved toward the table. Richard was afraid she would plop a bit of the cake into his mouth, and he would choke helplessly. But instead she just coated her index finger with frosting and held it in front of his lips. Rather than licking the gooey stuff, he pretended to misunderstand and kissed her thumb. She blushed.

"Let's go home," he whispered softly but distinctly.

She hunched her shoulders and eyed him guiltily. As she knelt beside him, her expression reminded him of Heinz right after the dog had torn down the curtains.

"Oh, gosh, Richard. Didn't I tell you? I couldn't get any aides for the weekend. So I am having the wheelchair ambulance service pick you up and bring you over tomorrow morning.'' She penitently grabbed his armrest and gave him a pleading, little-girl, don't-be-mad look.

He stared at her. What was she saying? Were they married or not? "I come now or I don't come at all.''

"Oh, Richard. Be reasonable.''

"You want another annulment? Go catch the priest.''

He had wounded her and brought her close to tears. But she had to understand he was her husband, not some pet she could pick up for her temporary amusement.

She shrugged and rose to her feet. "I'll go ask Al if he thinks we can manage.'' Al was across the room staring vacantly at a fuse box.

Vernice was standing next to Richard, looking sympathetic. She didn't offer any solace now, but he recalled what she always used to say after propping him into some weird position. "We'll lick this sucker yet.''

He watched as Cheryl walked slowly back to him. She was smiling—a favorable sign.

"Al thinks he can get you in the car,'' she said. "Shall we get your stuff?''

Richard gave Vernice a triumphant look. *I ain't licked. I ain't licked. I ain't licked.*

Chapter Nine

Rose liked being alone in the house. The solitary state sharpened her senses—made the wind sound stronger, the kitchen sink drip louder, and time pass more obviously so that she could almost hear a celestial tick tock.

She tightened the kitchen faucet, then straightened the rag rug in front of the sink. The braided mat had been made by her mother, and Rose could recognize bits of material from many of her childhood dresses—the green kettle cloth, the red gingham, the yellow and white striped. At fifteen the appealing part of that striped dress had been the thick yellow plastic belt that accompanied it. But apart from the belt her memories of the dress were not all that pleasant. She had a vivid recollection of wearing it at a dance where she had been too tall for every boy in her high-school gym. Too stupid to go home, she had stood alone at the place where the wrestling mats were hung and counted every visible stripe in that dress. Since Rose was neither a reminiscer nor a saver of slights, she supposed she had kept this incident fresh to share with Cheryl. But there had been no need. Her daughter had come home in tears from junior high dances and run straight into her father's arms. "You look sweet as candy," he would reassure her; though, in fact, she had been a lumpy, lethargic child who should have been advised to cultivate scholarly qualities or charm-school allure.

Now, that was a mean thought, Rose decided as she plunked down two thick quilted place mats on the butcher

block table. There was no sense in blaming the problems
of the living on the defenseless dead. Cheryl's predica-
ment was no more George's fault than her own. Rose
pulled out paper napkins, then the plain white plates
Cheryl had given her as a wedding gift. Al disliked an
accumulation of unnecessary silverware, so at each place
setting she put only one knife, one spoon, and one fork.
Which was funny because George, her first husband,
proclaimed himself unable to enjoy dinner without two
forks and a frosted water goblet. But what Rose found
even more amazing than these contrasts was that she, an
overly tall, rigidly Catholic woman, would have acquired
two husbands with which to make them.

The grandfather clock chimed five, and Rose re-
checked her list, which was long. This was one of those
rare Saturdays spent alone, and she tried to accomplish
a lot. First she had written the day's necessary activities
in a column on the back of a used envelope, printing at
the top: DO EXERCISES. And she had, before eating breakfast. Stretching and twisting to a record was a pleasant
activity in Al's absence. But when he was standing in the
kitchen doorway watching, she not only felt foolish rolling on the floor but patronized by the silky-voiced com-
mentator: "5-6-7-8-9. Twist your waist. You're doing
fine. Good girl."

Sometimes Rose wished she hadn't given Cheryl her
condominium. It would have eliminated a certain strain
in her marriage to be able to stop at the empty house, do
her exercises, then pluck her eyebrows in the well-lighted
upstairs bedroom. But now her only option was to pursue
private matters when Al was occupied elsewhere.

Today he had taken a temporary job with a logging
concern. Since the work was totally dependent on natural
light, she expected him home at any minute, which was
okay because the casserole was warmed and the garlic
bread was ready to pop into the oven.

In the refrigerator was a second casserole covered with
aluminum foil, ready to be taken to Cheryl's. Rose con-

sidered food the most appreciated gift when there was a sick person in the house, so she had also made up a batch of chocolate chip cookies. The cookies were now packed in a fruitcake container that her daughter would never remember to return. But let her keep it. The girl had been forced to pack up and return all the wedding gifts after Stu left her. At least the ceremony had been small. And the presents given to Cheryl at this last marriage were so dreadful no one would expect her to return them.

When she heard Al's truck grinding its way up their steep drive, she slid the garlic bread into the oven. He set his chain saw on its shelf in the garage before entering the kitchen. "How was it?" she asked. But he was still slightly deaf from working near the chipper at the mill and did not answer—just smiled before going to shower off a day's accumulation of sweat and sawdust. Thank God, she thought, that I haven't been waiting all day to talk to him.

She got out Al's beer, then poured herself a glass of wine. Though Rose had now been married for a year and a half, Cheryl still thought Al's reticence toward her implied animosity. She couldn't accept that Al wasn't a talker; Cheryl apparently never noticed that whatever Rose asked him ("Why did the muffler have to fall off the car right there? How could those parents treat a child like that?"), he always gave the same brief answer: "Just the nature of the beast, I guess."

Though Rose had to admit Al's conversational skills were undernourished, he sometimes displayed an old-fashioned delicacy she found touching. Since no amount of scrubbing could completely erase the grease stains from his hands, he was shy about touching the common food. So when he appeared with hair still wet from his shower, she broke off several chunks of garlic bread and set them on his plate.

"Thanks." And then staring dreamily at a spot over her right shoulder, he said, "Lou Hazen got his foot smashed today."

Smashed might mean bruised, broken, or worse. As she had a queasy stomach, she was temporarily grateful for his vagueness. Any medical discussion would have destroyed her appetite, which wasn't much to begin with. She ate what she could and then waited for him.

When Al was through, Rose got up for the coffee, then went to the refrigerator for milk. She watched him staring at the familiar blue and white container.

"It's buttermilk," he said.

She flushed and slapped her hand against her forehead. "Oh, Lord. I'm getting blind as a bat. Must have bought it because the package is the same color as the regular."

"It's okay. I'll mix up some of the powdered stuff."

She knew he was being deliberately casual about this incident and felt doubly humiliated by his kindness. Had they been the same age she could have accepted it. But he was thirty-eight and couldn't possibly know what it felt like to have failing vision, hot flashes, and a permanently stiff neck. His hair was still wavy, thick, and black—while she had to work with a hot comb every morning to coax life into her tinted coif.

And her vision *was* getting bad. This afternoon she had stood on tiptoe in front of the bathroom mirror with its tiny sausage-shaped light bulbs and, using her old bifocals as a monocle, tried to tweeze her eyebrows.

After all that effort they were still straggly. She knew he would install an overhead light if she asked him, but she also knew she could never ask. It would make her feel too pathetic.

If only she had anticipated how quickly she would begin to age after fifty, she might never have married him. But there had been very little anticipation and absolutely no reason involved. At forty-nine, her hormones had betrayed her and left her with sex drives so unbecoming to her age and widowed state, she often mentally compared herself to a piece of rotting fruit—an abandoned orange, turned moldy green and oozing its vital juices. When the school bus driver, Al Valerino, had asked her to dinner, she felt foolish for wanting so badly to accept. Al reminded her of the dark-eyed, swarthy boys she had admired in high school. *Bronx imports*, her Yankee father had called them.

But in Al's case, he would have been wrong. The senior Valerinos had moved to Fairfield County from Queens. "Why here?" she asked him on that first date. "My dad came up to the state fair and thought it was pretty country," he answered, and touched his wineglass to hers.

After that he became disturbingly quiet, and she began to babble nervously. "Did you know it was Charlemagne who is supposed to have initiated the toast? He felt that drinking involved all the senses but hearing. I don't know if there is any truth in that. It came from my husband, and he was a lawyer."

"Were you happy being married?"

He asked so innocently and wistfully, she felt she owed him more than a defensive *of course*. "Yes and no. It's a lot of work. Sometimes you just feel like you're on a treadmill. I was always making lists, always so regimented. There was this bound set of Shakespeare's plays in our bedroom, and I thought when I got some time I'd read them and try writing some poetry. But after George died, I hadn't the patience for Shakespeare and though I still wrote lists, I never wrote any poetry. So I don't know if I lost the capacity for solitary thought or if I just never had it." She had no idea whether he understood or not, but three weeks later he proposed, and the only hurdle left had been telling Cheryl.

Oh, God. They still had to go over to Cheryl's disorganized house tonight. The very thought of that mess made her neck ache. She lifted her hand to rub it.

"You tired?" Al asked.

"No. I just need to wash up and we can go."

"Leave the dishes. We'll get them tonight."

She was about to argue. The dishes did not take ten minutes and she hated to leave them dirty, but he was already standing and impatiently shifting his weight from one leather work shoe to the other. She grabbed her sweater and followed him out to the car.

On the short trip to Cheryl's she concentrated on her back. Rose had discovered it eased tension to pretend her spinal column was composed of building blocks that needed individual realignment. By the time she had mentally reached the top block, they were nearing the town line on old Route 6 and just passing the Connecticut Court Motel.

The arc of dilapidated cabins had been built some twenty-five years ago as a honeymoon haven for New Yorkers unable to afford the Cape. Now the white bungalows with their peeling paint and sagging porches reminded her of decaying teeth; they looked like a place where you might go to commit suicide. Rose shivered and draped her sweater around her shoulders. She was getting ghoulish and knew why. In just a few minutes she was going to have to face that sick boy again. She had nothing prepared to say to him. What was there to say to someone who would never walk or lead a useful, productive life again?

When she had first met Richard, she had focused on his innocent face. That made her feel hopeful. If Cheryl wanted to devote herself to assisting Richard, she had no objections. His recuperation was certainly a more worthwhile goal than those idiotic diets she generally embraced. Besides, at first Richard reminded her of those fair-haired boys with dogs in Walt Disney movies. It was not apparent until six days ago, when Cheryl brought him home, how helpless and hopelessly infirm he was. At least, it had not been apparent to Rose. Al had known and tried to coax her into stopping the wedding. But when she stated her reluctance to interfere, he withdrew his protests. Now she wished he had been more resolute about his misgivings. But he was never very resolute. He even hesitated to voice his opinion on a made-for-TV movie until he knew whether she liked it or not.

* * *

More than twenty years ago some guidance counselor had branded him as "not college material" and the scars still ran deep. If only she could communicate to him what little impact higher education had made on her own life. Her four years had left her with vague memories of behavioral objectives in Education 101, a few useless French phrases, and the faded program from her graduation ceremony. College had not endowed her with any magical qualities for effective decision making or left her with a coherent scheme for making sense of the events in her life. But she could not tell him that. They did not have those kinds of conversations.

Rose looked over at her husband. He always drove with slumped shoulders and a fierce, withdrawn expression—like some animal expecting attack at any moment. His right knuckles held the wheel at the twelve o'clock position. His left hand rested palm open on his jean-clad thigh. It was not the posture recommended by driving instructors, but he was by far the best driver she had ever known. She watched as he signaled and pulled into Constitution Square.

There was no guest parking available near Cheryl's condo, so they left the truck in another section of the development and walked through the parking lot. Al carried the casserole in one hand and held her wrist with the other. If Cheryl hadn't been able to find a nurse's aide to care for Richard, Al would have to help the boy to get up, bathe, and shave. It was a physically and emotionally difficult job, but it never occurred to him to complain. She looped her fingers through his and squeezed. There was nothing to say.

Cheryl opened the door before they even reached the front steps. She was wearing an unflattering horizontally striped T-shirt. Her hair looked as if it hadn't been washed since the wedding.

Al set the casserole on the kitchen counter while Cheryl cowered and said, "He's been in bed all day. I called all the agencies but none of them had an aide to send.'' She waited there anxiously, penitently, as if she were expecting Al to make some pronouncement on her actions. But he just shrugged and went directly to Richard.

Rose placed the cookies beside the casserole, then peered through the kitchen entryway into the living room. Al had pulled the wheelchair up to Richard's bedside and was talking gently to the boy, who lay motionless in the big hospital bed. "How are you feeling? Watching some television? I'm going to rub your leg and arm to loosen them up a bit.'' Al shed his nylon windbreaker without dropping a syllable. "Are you feeling kind of stiff? Is this helping? Is the leg looser? How about now? The arm okay? Ready?'' Then Al put his left arm behind the boy's back, his right under Richard's knees, and with one swift, graceful movement swung him into a sitting position. For the last four nights Rose had watched in awe. She knew Al had been a medic in Vietnam, but before Richard's arrival she had never seen him demonstrate his skill with the disabled.

Cheryl tugged at her arm. "Let's go upstairs.''

Rose jammed her hands into the pockets of her skirt and reluctantly followed her daughter up the carpeted stairs. She needed to talk to Cheryl but would have preferred remaining in the entryway watching Al. There was something very touching about one man helping another.

When they got to the top of the stairs, Rose peered wistfully into her old master bedroom with its huge walk-in closet. The room was unused now; Cheryl had chosen to remain in the small bedroom. Giving her daughter the condo had been a foolish, emotional gesture. But Rose had been so grateful to Cheryl for hosting a shower and supervising the wedding arrangements. Cheryl had just been deserted by Stu at the time, and Rose had thought in wonder: she must love me; she really must love me to be doing this. But after going to that farce of a wedding at the nursing home, Rose realized it was just the ceremony itself that her daughter loved.

Cheryl's bedroom set and desk were yellow. Her chair was a high-backed wicker throne. All the furniture was built on a preteen scale that made Rose feel like an Amazon. She carefully lowered herself into the wicker chair while Cheryl slumped on her bed. Rose eyed the frilly coverlet and thought: well, at least she made her bed today.

Cheryl pointed to the bulging envelope purse on the dresser next to her mother. "Pass me a cigarette."

Rose lifted the purse and fished out the cigarettes. As she passed them over, she noticed the stack of romance novels on the bedside table. Cheryl had obviously spent her day reading British fiction about poor shopgirls who drank tea, smoked fags, and married well. Rose slumped back in the wicker chair and gripped the armrests. There was a very sick boy downstairs. If her daughter ever needed to deal with reality, now was the time.

Cheryl grabbed the dime-store glass ashtray from her desk. "Gosh, Mom. I don't know what to do. Richard's regressed to the way he was when I started visiting him. He doesn't eat. He doesn't talk. I can't keep a nurse's aide because he gets so nasty."

So that explained her retreat into fantasy. The important thing was to be sympathetic and not make her feel defensive. "You've taken on an impossible job. The boy needs constant care. The nursing home might be able to better provide—"

"*Boy!*" Cheryl half stood, half slid off the bed. "Just because Richard is ill! He's twenty-nine, Mom. He's an adult; he's a man. And that nursing home packed up his belongings in a garbage bag when he left. He had to leave with a black garbage bag. I will never send him back there." She started to cry. First there was an artificial sob, and then she managed to squeeze out two real tears. "Being sick from a stroke is just like being a secretary. You cease to be a person, a grown-up. *I'll have my girl call your girl.*"

Oh, Lord, Rose thought, here she goes. She could

never understand why Cheryl did not return to school and train for something else if she found her job so demeaning. But George had brought her up to believe she was a princess—that all good things were her birthright. She didn't know how to work for anything. There I go blaming George again. It's my fault, too. I never understood what she needed.

Rose remembered a six-year-old Cheryl standing by her side and wailing "I haven't got anything to do." At the same age Rose had loaded up all her dolls on her big brass bed, looped a rope through the headboard, then drove her covered wagon through hostile Indian territory. And she had lined up the dining room chairs and pretended to be a train conductor. When she had suggested similar pursuits to Cheryl, the child constantly wailed "What do I do next? What do I do next?" Rose had not known how to entertain a child with no interests and no imagination.

Cheryl stood. "Shall we go check on our *men*?"

Rose had been a teacher for too long to react to childish outbursts. "Okay. I need to refrigerate that casserole, too."

She thrust the dish into the refrigerator, then stared in amazement at the mess on the kitchen table. It looked as if her entire class of kindergartners had been let loose in the kitchen. There was an oversize dishpan full of scummy water with shaving cream heaped on one side. Beside that was a mirror, a razor, a comb, a glass, an uncapped toothpaste container, a toothbrush, and a kidney-shaped bowl.

Al and Richard were back in the living room in front of the TV. Rose followed her daughter into the room. "You made a mess," she told her husband. Then realizing she had not yet acknowledged Richard, she smiled and said, "How are you? Been watching TV?" Richard smelled of lime shaving lotion and looked more emaciated than ever.

Neither question was very original, but when he did

not answer, she flushed and turned to her husband with a pleading look, meaning: *can we soon get out of here?* She felt too tall, too awkward, too unwelcome. And then from behind her a deep voice said, "Situation comedies mostly." Startled, she turned and stared at Richard, who was giving her a dazzling smile. From his wheelchair he had gallantly rescued her from feeling ugly and unwanted, and for a moment she half understood why Cheryl had married him. He looked so boyish and hopeful that she was reluctant for their conversation to end. "You didn't have a TV at the—" She flushed, then tactfully substituted *hospital* for *nursing home.*

"No."

He was still focusing his celebrity grin on her, and Rose smiled back in gratitude. "Did you forget what it was like?"

"Yeah, but it comes back fast. Sort of like the scent of cheap cologne."

What an apt analogy. Rose turned to see if Cheryl was appreciating it, but she wore a cross, petulant look. *He won't talk to me. He's talking to my mother.*

I'd like to get him out of here, Rose decided. Take him to our place for a while. Al could nurse him. I could get him books from the library. He and I could talk. Then suddenly Richard was tired. His mouth sagged; his eyes rolled. Cheryl's sullen expression changed to fright.

Al put his hand on the boy's back. "Tired?" he asked kindly, then lifted Richard back into bed.

Rose, embarrassed by her son-in-law's near-nakedness, pretended to be fastening the decorative buckle on her clog. When Richard was comfortably settled, Al looked at her and stated without his usual hesitancy, "We better go." Al was more decisive around Richard, which confirmed that her decision to bring the boy home would benefit everybody. Then Rose looked at her still-frightened daughter and thought: what am I doing? How could she think about taking over her daughter's husband? It was sick. She glanced at the hospital bed and the enormous metal device the nurses' aides used to lift Richard. It was all sick. Some unfortunate marriages might end in this state, but she was sure no other had started this way.

She strolled over by Richard's bed to wish him good night, then bent down as if picking up a tissue and ran her hand down the wall above the baseboard. Memory served her well. There was a telephone jack just behind the bed. I will have a phone installed there tomorrow, she decided. I'll call it a belated wedding present; then I'll coax Al into going away for a week. She had amassed twenty-five years of devoted service at the Ridgely school system and knew the principal wouldn't begrudge her some extra time off. She and Al might drive up to Cranberry Lake. Al could fish. And Cheryl, when forced to deal with this situation alone, would realize how impossible it was. The plan sounded logical and less harsh than letting a dangerous situation continue. Besides, if things got too bad during that week, Richard could always make a phone call. Her daughter would hate her, but Rose was sure she did already.

Chapter Ten

Cheryl stared out the kitchen window at the rain. If it had not been for Richard's fragile lungs, she could have taken some satisfaction in the damp spring weather. She hoped Rose and Al were having a rotten time in upstate New York—all chilled and huddled together. Then it occurred to her that other people had sex lives and were less inconvenienced by inclement weather. I will not cry, she told herself, as she paced back and forth on her tiny kitchen floor, staring at the checkered linoleum. I won't cry. I won't cry. The Home Health Agency was sending a supervisory nurse, and after she got here everything would be all right.

There was so much information she needed to give the nurse—like how Richard was not eating. Unless there was some change this morning. She padded into the living room in her gown and terrycloth scuffs to check his tray. The circle of brown sugar on top of his Cream of Wheat was unbroken, which meant he had not even tried it. Nor had he eaten any of the applesauce. She lifted the tray and asked, "Could I bring you something else?"

He shook his head no.

Cheryl carried the tray back to the kitchen. For the last two weeks most of her energy had gone into cooking soft foods. All of which he had rejected. She felt more like an unwanted waitress than a wife.

She dumped the applesauce down the drain, then stared longingly at the Cream of Wheat. It was cool, but the brown sugar smelled nice. How many calories in Cream of Wheat? Lots, probably. She quickly spooned the cereal down the drain, ran cold water, and flipped on the disposal switch. Black coffee was calorieless. She poured herself half a cup and, feeling slightly virtuous, ran upstairs with it.

A shower would feel good, but there was no time. The nurse might be here at any moment. Cheryl put on jeans and a turtleneck shirt and exchanged her worn scuffs for new elasticized slippers. Then she went back downstairs and returned to staring out the window.

The garbageman came. He pulled his green truck into the empty spaces beside her Vega and, with much grinding of gears, backed over to the Dempster Dumpster. The curly-haired driver had to emerge from the truck to pick up some papers and boxes lying outside the trash container. He hurled them inside with angry, jabbing motions as if their presence were a personal affront. When he hopped back into the cab, a shrill, grating noise started. Then two long metal prongs slid under the dumpster and lifted it high in the air. A day's worth of Constitution Square's garbage cascaded into the back of the truck.

The whole process reminded her of that Hoyer lift the nurse's aides used on Richard. First they slid under him a parachutelike nylon sling, which was fastened by chain links to the hanger of a tall metal contraption on wheels. Richard was then pumped into a sitting position, causing him to resemble an enormous baby in the clutches of a mechanical stork. But no baby ever cursed like he did. And no aide ever came back a second time. Maybe this new agency had more stouthearted employees.

She peeked into the living room. Richard's breathing sounded bubbly and raspy, like her mother's old glass coffee percolator. Fluid was collecting in his lungs, and he needed to be sitting up. The nurse had better get here soon. She stared at the beige wall phone. She ate half a banana as she watched a puddle collect in the parking lot. At eleven o'clock she called the agency. The dispatcher told her Mrs. Elter had six new cases to evaluate and would arrive sometime between nine and three.

"I thought they told me morning," Cheryl said apologetically, knowing full well they had told her morning but not wanting to antagonize anyone. This was the only home care agency left in Fairfield County.

How could her mother and Al have left right now? How?

To banish her tears she again checked on Richard. "Can I do anything?" He looked stiff, starved, uncomfortable, but he shook his head no. She emptied his plastic urinal, which he had set as far away from him as possible—right by that useless red phone her mother had sent. Who did she think he was going to call? Dumb, dumb, dumb, she thought, as she swished Lysol in the urinal, then replaced it by the phone. She switched on the TV for him. It was the best she could do.

At 12:30 she fixed him tomato soup and a grilled cheese sandwich. At one o'clock she dumped the cold soup and ate the rejected sandwich herself. She gulped it down guiltily while standing by the stove. She didn't want the nurse to catch her stuffing herself. In fact, she had never much liked anyone watching her eat. During her early teens she had breakfasted daintily, eating only the egg white and half a piece of toast. Then she would take the Entenmann's coffee cake up to her bedroom and eat the entire thing, sliding the incriminating container under her bed.

Finally armies of ants converged on her bedroom and her mother attacked with a spray can of Raid. Cheryl had waited to be slapped, scolded, punished. But Rose remained calm. "Amazing," she had said, "the way these little creatures got all the way upstairs." For Rose to display anger, Cheryl supposed, would have betrayed too close a connection to that fat, hopeless child. You had to love someone to yell at her.

An elderly shriveled man carrying an oversize black umbrella walked by the window. She watched him go as far as the brick gate, where he stopped to wait for the bus. Cheryl wanted to offer him her car keys but doubted that he drove. Since she could not help, she felt obligated to continue leaning against the cold aluminum sink watching until the city bus stopped for him.

Shortly after that the nurse parked her compact car in the spot where the garbage truck had been. Mrs. Elter wore a blue raincoat, had limp gray hair, and looked, Cheryl thought with relief, motherly. She also appeared to be familiar with the layout of Constitution Square condominiums, for she proceeded directly to the kitchen and set a worn leather satchel on the table. Cheryl took her damp coat, then gestured to the living room. "Richard is in there."

Mrs. Elter pulled a yellow file folder from her satchel and sat down at the table. "I'd like to ask you a few questions first, Mrs. Olsen," she said kindly. "If you don't mind. And then I'll speak to Mr. Olsen."

Cheryl nodded. "Oh, sure." It was such a relief to have somebody capable tell her what to do. But the kitchen furniture had been rearranged to accommodate Richard's wheelchair and now the other chair was at the far end of the table. Cheryl tried to move it, but succeeded only in knocking over a return-for-deposit Coke bottle that was by the wastebasket. She blushed and sat down. "I've gotten a little behind in my housework."

Mrs. Elter smiled sympathetically. "That's perfectly understandable." The yellow file folder had inside pockets. Just like a kangaroo, Cheryl thought, choking down a giggle. She did not want Mrs. Elter to think she was hysterical. The nurse pulled a mimeographed sheet from a pocket and smoothed it out. "How old is your husband, Mrs. Olsen?"

"Twenty-nine."

The woman made a clucking sound. "And how long ago did the aneurysm occur?"

"Sixteen months ago. Richard could tell you better about all that. We weren't married then."

Mrs. Elter ceased writing. "How long have you been married?"

"Eleven days."

"Oh, I see."

The woman did not see at all. She developed a guarded look as if she suddenly realized she was dealing with an obvious oddball. Her sympathy was replaced by a distant professionalism. "Well, everything seems to be in order. I need to take Mr. Olsen's temperature and blood pressure. When was his last BM?"

Cheryl gulped. "I don't know. I mean, it's not something we've discussed." She gestured into the living room. "Richard would know better. My stepfather enlarged the door on the downstairs bathroom so Richard's wheelchair could fit in. But he's away."

Mrs. Elter stood. "Let me examine Mr. Olsen."

Baffled, Cheryl remained at the kitchen table. Richard was depressed. He refused to talk or eat. So did it really matter when he last had a bowel movement? Apparently it did, for Mrs. Elter was back within minutes to announce: "I'm going to have to administer an enema. I could use some plastic sheets. A dry cleaner's bag would do."

"Does that need to be done first? He hasn't eaten anything. And he hasn't had a bath or sat up."

"The aides feed and bathe him. They can't do this, though, and it was ordered by his doctor at the Home."

"Oh, I see." With fleeting self-pity Cheryl decided that a college dropout like herself had no right to question a professional. After ripping two plastic bags off never-worn spring suits, she went upstairs into her bedroom and closed the door. Too agitated to read, she sat in the wicker chair and stared at the paperback romance on her dresser.

"Cheryl. Cheryl." Even through the closed door, she could hear Richard's importunate cries. It was the first time in several days he had wanted her, and she could not go to him. If only her husband had continued to need her and love her, they might have made a go of it. Instead he had retreated into his own private world, and this marriage, just like her first, was slipping through her fingers.

She got up, turned on the radio, and flipped from station to station, but that did not prevent her from hearing Richard's anguished scream. "No. No. No! Go away. For God's sake, go away!"

Cheryl hoisted herself out of the chair and started running downstairs. Her perspiring feet stuck to the foam soles of her slippers. She had not worn shoes in four days and felt dirty, unkempt, lifeless. The lethargy left her when she got to the base of the stairs and saw Mrs. Elter shaking her husband's arm.

"Calm yourself," the nurse ordered Richard.

Cheryl clenched her fists and straightened. "Please leave, Mrs. Elter."

The woman's face and neck turned splotchy red. "I thought you wanted help."

"We do want help. My husband wants to be made more comfortable. I don't see you doing that." Though Cheryl had never dismissed anyone before, her voice remained calm and firm. To this nurse Richard was not a man, just a collection of ailments, and Cheryl wanted her out of their home as quickly as possible. She was relieved when the woman began stuffing her medical paraphernalia back into her nurse's bag.

"I need you to initial my visit sheet, Mrs. Olsen."

Cheryl used the magnetized pen that clung to the refrigerator to scribble her initials, then she went immediately to Richard. Generally she was embarrassed to display concern and affection for her husband in front of these medical people, but today she took Richard's hand and held it tenderly.

She heard Mrs. Elter mutter "I'm way behind in my schedule" as she banged out the front door.

When Cheryl went back to the kitchen and peered out the window, she noticed there was a green puddle where Mrs. Elter's car had been. Her car is leaking antifreeze,

Cheryl noted cheerfully. She then stared at the linen calendar that next year could be used as a dish towel. Now that the weekday and weekend routine never varied, she paid little attention to dates. But tomorrow something was happening. Heinz! Jetlag Johnson was putting him on a plane bound from Florida into LaGuardia. Someone had to stay with Richard while she drove to the airport. But who? Mrs. Elter's agency certainly wouldn't send an aide for tomorrow.

That witch of a nurse had probably reached the Interstate by now. And Rose was staying at some rustic cabin where the only phone was at the motel office. Everyone has deserted me, Cheryl thought as her eyes began to tear.

She shook her head savagely. "Stop it. Stop it," she admonished herself. Richard needed her to be calm right now. However bad she must feel, he must feel worse. And with that realization, she returned to his room.

"Richard, are you all right? I'm sorry about that woman. I'll never let her come again." She rubbed his back with long rhythmic strokes. He had become so gaunt and frail this last week. Leaving him to Mrs. Elter's devices would have been like throwing a baby bird in front of a truck. Richard appeared to be asleep, but she was not certain, so she knelt beside his bed. "I'm very sorry." She wished he would acknowledge her once before she had to send him away. But first she wanted to give him a chance to see his dog.

The phone rang, and Cheryl ran to it with relief. It was just like that adage: always darkest before the dawn. Rose and Al had come home early. Everything was going to be all right. They could stay with Richard until she got back from the airport and then help her get him admitted to the hospital.

But the soft childish voice was not her mother's. It was Lucy's. "Cheryl, I can't find Mr. Derrigo's customer files for Europe."

She took a deep breath, tried to remember where the

chronological files were. ''The cabinet by the water fountain. Third drawer down.''

"Hold on." And then: "I don't see it."

"It has a red tab."

"Oh, I found it," Lucy said happily. "How is everything going?"

"Fine."

"Lucky you not to be working."

Cheryl hung up the phone, then walked over to the
counter and lifted the top off the tin of homemade cookies her mother had brought. The oval lid was decorated
with a still-life mural of clay crockery, one bowl containing fresh cherries with stiff stems. She set down the
top, then stared down into the tin. The cookies were
lumpy with chocolate chips and nothing Richard would
be interested in. Cheryl decided to eat just one.

Chapter Eleven

Richard spent a lot of time thinking about his grandmother. During his preschool days, he had spent most of his time waiting for her. Each day after his mother went to work, Grandma would coax him into action with the promise of a trip to the park. He got dressed, tied his new blue sneakers as best he could, and waited. Then in boredom he rolled his socks up and down and picked at his mosquito bites. Finally he went to check on her.

She was generally standing in front of her bedroom mirror wearing a yellowed slip and flapping her flabby arms up and down like some mammoth bird about to ascend. "My deodorant isn't dry," she would explain. When he had abandoned all hope of leaving their hot one-bedroom apartment and had settled in front of an *I Love Lucy* rerun, she would appear in the living room to ask "Aren't you ready yet, pumpkin?"

His grandmother had been the dominant influence on his young life because his mother was totally preoccupied with self-improvement. She usually stayed in West Palm Beach after work and ate at the diner because she was enrolled in a Dale Carnegie course or attended an art appreciation class or an Arthur Murray dance lesson. But on Wednesdays she bowled, which caused Richard to suspect that merely keeping away from their too-small apartment was a prime motivator in her constant quest for improvement.

Regardless, his days rolled along with regularity. While his grandmother rested he spent the hot afternoons throwing a tennis ball against the brick wall of their apartment building. He always came back at 4:30 because he knew she would have set a plate of Ritz crackers smeared with pimento spread on the glass-topped coffee table. It was cocktail time and while he drank ginger ale from a juice glass, she had a manhattan with two cherries.

At six o'clock they ate supper. They usually had pork and beans or canned spaghetti. Because Richard was a growing child, there was a salad and a dish of canned fruit cocktail set to the side of his plate. Grandma liked cans because they spared her from ever having to touch the food. Even the cherry tomatoes in his salad had come from a Winn-Dixie can. Grandma would spoon the plump tomatoes onto the lettuce, then sprinkle the salad with dehydrated onions that had been soaking in the shot glass.

After supper she always carried her coffee into her bedroom to say the rosary. Sometimes she misplaced her mug and had to summon him. He would shift through the jumble of magazines, jewelry, and glow-in-the-dark statues on her dresser until he found the still-warm mug. Then she gratefully patted his arm. "You're a good boy, Richie," she would proclaim confidently. "A good, good boy."

As he approached school age his mother began to take a more active interest in his life. She signed him up for the Pee-Wee Softball League. His athletic coordination might already have been apparent, or she may have observed that her son and her mother were becoming isolated in their oddness. But if she intended to change him, she was too late. He had already developed a permanent preference for canned food and solitude.

Cheryl ventured to the door of Richard's room and gave him an anxious look. She periodically walked by to see if he was still alive. Besides turning him from side to side and emptying his urinal that was all she could do.

Despite her lack of nursing skills she had profoundly changed his way of thinking.

Before coming here he had been convinced there was a national organization of women whose goal was to make him suffer. In an attempt to make peace with the enemy he had married this woman; but the torturing continued. Cheryl merely hired other women to do it.

Surely his bride didn't wish him harm. To be capable of intentional evil, a person needed to be blindly complacent and have absolute convictions; but Cheryl regretted her every act five minutes after its completion. Therefore, Richard concluded, she had to believe these people helped him. These cruel acts must be perpetrated upon all sick people. If that was the case, then there was no national conspiracy, no enemy to fight, and consequently no reason to live. Starving could take a long time but, fortunately, some sticky substance was wrapping itself around his lungs the way Spanish moss engulfed the weeping willows down South. Maybe it wouldn't take so long.

Cheryl sat on the floor and looked up into his face. He absolutely hated when she did that. It was unfortunate that he had gotten involved with her, but he had not understood the hopelessness of his situation until after they were married. He wished he had married Janey Birch. He kept coming back to that the way one probes a sore tooth. But it was too late for regrets. It was too late for everything.

"I am such a pig. Do you know what I just did?"

He was dying, and she was confessing. It made no sense. He stared past her, stared through the sliding glass doors and out into the untended patio. The bricks composing the floor were made of a decorative fleur-de-lis pattern, but he had no desire to count them.

"I ate a whole tin of cookies." She brushed her hand against the rug. "I don't know why I did that. I've been so good up until now. I didn't eat your Cream of Wheat, and it really smelled good. All I had all day was coffee, a banana, and a sandwich. Then I blew it. God, I'm worthless.''

Was she asking for comfort? Forgiveness? Either way he was completely unequal to the task. He did perform one feat of gallantry for her, but he doubted she was aware of it. His hand shook so that using the urinal without spillage was difficult, but he hoped he could continue managing it up until the end.

"I should have cooked a balanced meal for us. I would eat more sensibly if you were eating something. I should have cooked chili. Except for the kidney beans, chili is very low-calorie. But you don't eat ground beef, do you?''

He raised his right hand in a reflexive, protective gesture, but the bombardment of words continued. He stopped listening. How could she accuse him of not eating ground beef? He had almost completely subsisted on White Castle hamburgers from his sophomore through senior years of high school. After his grandmother died his mother started coming home after work. But he was intent on revenge and he never made it home in time for dinner. When questioned, he would plead practices to attend, game films to review, laps to swim. This cruelty might have been passed on from generation to generation, except now there would be no next generation.

Cheryl, defeated by his inattention, adjusted the TV, then let him be. She reappeared later to give him some cough syrup, which had a thick, cherry taste. She plunked the bottle on his table. "I'll leave it here in case you need it later.'' When she patted his arm, her hand felt warm and dry.

Her hands still felt warm when she touched his forehead that night. Seeing her pendulous breasts and thick silhouette, he thought he was again being caressed by his grandmother and he fell back into a dreamless, secure sleep.

Chapter Twelve

Cheryl was a masterful driver. She maneuvered the Saw Mill Parkway, the Hutch, and Interstate 84 with equal ease. Driving had never worried her, but she had always been terrified of dogs. She could not see Heinz in her rearview mirror. Even so, there was too much potential danger involved to forget he was there. At any moment the dog might jump up and bite her neck or leap into the front seat and stick its damp, licorice-colored nose into the crotch of her lime slacks. Cheryl shuddered and gripped the steering wheel tighter. She was afraid to turn the radio on. There was no telling what effect music might have on the creature. It was best to stay calm and speak softly. "We've just passed White Plains, Heinz, and now we're getting onto 684. In a half hour we'll be with Richard. You remember Richard?"

That sounded both idiotic and patronizing; but perhaps she was merely being boring, for Heinz yawned. She could hear his formidable teeth click closed. She had paid a limousine driver whose fare had not arrived twenty dollars to walk Heinz from the luggage area to the car. The dog had been orderly enough, and Cheryl watched the somberly dressed young driver, relieved she did not have to speculate on his marital status or potential earning power. In fact, she did not have to do anything but pay him. This was no once-in-a-lifetime fateful encounter. She was a married woman now. A *married woman*. But after the man left she again became simply terrified. She was alone in her Vega with a dog, a very big dog.

When they arrived at the condo, she opened the back car door. Still reluctant to touch him, she commanded, "Get out, Heinz." The dog slid just far enough forward so that its head prevented her from closing the door. She stared down at his black toenails, worn white at the tips, and wondered what to do. If she went to check on Richard, the dog might leap from the car and never be found again. But Richard had been left alone for nearly four hours. She tentatively pulled on the metal leash. When Heinz did not budge, she got out her car keys and edged forward to open the front door.

It felt as if the bathroom rug brushed by her knees, but it was the dog, pushing past her and running toward the living room. "Stop. Stop!" He shouldn't do that, Cheryl reasoned. Richard was too ill for surprises. She lunged forward, but her purse strap caught in the door latch, and by the time she had disentangled herself, the dog was already on the hospital bed. The side rails had been no deterrent at all. He had simply leapt forward from the base of the bed and was now licking Richard's face. Oh, God, the germs.

But they were regarding each other so tenderly, she thought it best not to interfere. Heinz was kind of pretty. His coat was composed of the colors carpet salesmen show samples of: tawny, rusty brown, champagne, and golden brown. Richard looked like a child on Christmas morning as his large-knuckled hand began to caress the dog's side. She waited there proudly, impatient to tell him about the effort involved in locating Heinz. But Richard continued stroking the panting dog, apparently requiring no explanation for the creature's miraculous presence. The invisible woman—that's what she was. Whatever she did, it wasn't enough to capture anyone's approval. Her bosses misunderstood her. Waitresses never remembered to take her order. Husbands forgot her. She stomped off to the kitchen to make herself some instant coffee.

She had stood by a similar stove on the day after her

wedding to Stu, drinking black coffee and crying herself sick. She had been brought up to believe that scraped knees were followed by lemon sherbet. But nothing happened except nightfall, so she washed her bloated face, put on one of the nightgowns she had intended to take on her honeymoon, and went to bed.

The teakettle began to whistle. Cheryl dumped the boiling water into her mug and began to relive her marriage day with Stu. She rehashed this incident so often that now the process of memory was barely involved. It was more like slamming a tape into a cassette. Detail after detail came to mind as effortlessly as listening to canned music.

It had all begun in the morning. Stuart had called Rose and told her he was not willing to go through with the wedding. That he called Rose just illustrated how hopeless it had all been. Since guests were already traveling, her practical mother advised him to attend the nuptials, cancel the honeymoon, and request an immediate annulment. Cheryl had come down the aisle on her mother's arm, thinking what a touching sight they were—and all the while Rose knew it was a joke.

On their wedding night Stu acted in a strictly professional capacity, not as a groom. Stu spoke rationally and offered her Valium, which she hurled across the room. The pills formed a green clump, which transfixed her while he tried to explain himself.

"It's like buying a shirt in the wrong size and hoping it will shrink or stretch. It's too big a gamble for us."

Whether she was too much woman for him or not enough, she never knew, for he quickly switched from the general to the specific. He had just run into an old girlfriend, whose name was June; he knew he still loved her. He spoke with an urgency that implied his intense feelings were completely unprecedented.

"June," Cheryl had repeated, "just like the month most people get married in." For a second or two he regarded her with his former soulful sympathy; but it was just a friendly gesture. By then she had lost him completely.

She had not even been allowed one solitary Saturday night to sit with her feet up and think about all those singles still out searching. Instead she was still single herself. At work she pretended to be a blissful newlywed. On her own time she paid a professional matchmaker four hundred dollars to fix her up with three so-called referrals. They were awful (all of them) and far more awkward than blind dates, because there were no shared friends to discuss and no common ground at all—except for disgust over the enormity of the matchmaker's fee. That perky blonde at One Plus One Dating was not the pay-later type, and Cheryl was pretty sure she charged women more than men. Nothing personal—just business, governed by supply and demand.

Cheryl sipped at her coffee, which was too strong. She wanted to add milk and sugar; that, however, would elevate the caloric total to an unacceptable sixty.

"Cheryl, Cheryl!" She took one more gulp and went back into the living room. The dog was down on his haunches now, lying beside Richard with his tawny, rusty brown, champagne, and golden brown feet stretched forward. Richard smiled at her shyly. It was the first he had acknowledged her in days and made her realize how vastly she had reduced her expectations in the last week. Now all she wanted was to let him enjoy his dog for a few hours.

"Heinz is hungry."

She clamped her hand to her mouth. "Dog food! I never bought any dog food. God, I'm a jerk. No cans, no biscuits. Nothing."

Richard gave her a tolerant, amused look. "Heinz doesn't like dog food. Do you have peanut butter?"

"Just the low-calorie kind."

"Could I get up?"

That request made her eyes water. He used to have entire grandstand crowds sitting on the edge of their seats, and now he needed her assistance in leaving bed. "Oh, sure," she replied bravely, though she was terrified of using the hydraulic lift. She wheeled the clanking machine over by his bed. "Could the dog get down?"

He patted the sheet. "Down, Heinz." The dog scampered off the bed and regarded her woefully. She rolled the nylon sling as if it were a diploma, then slid it under Richard. His back was sweaty. When she cranked him into a sitting position, he gagged up buckets of yellow phlegm.

"Oh, God," she whispered as she ran to the kitchen for paper towels.

Richard regarded the soaked front of his bedgown, then said calmly, "I'm all right." It was the dog he was trying to reassure, not her. Heinz was howling loudly, which made Cheryl more nervous. By the time she had Richard cleaned up and in the wheelchair, her hands shook, her legs quivered, and she was exhausted. God give me strength, she pleaded. She just wanted to give her husband one pleasant day with his dog.

She wheeled him into the kitchen, where Richard asked, "Could you get me the peanut butter, two slices of bread, and a knife, please." He spoke like a man accustomed to issuing polite orders. When she forgot the knife, he pointed to the open silverware drawer. His commanding directness was a sharp contrast to her own apologetic manner of requesting things. The uncomfortable thought crossed her mind that Richard had the potential for being very domineering. It didn't really worry her. He was going to the hospital shortly. What power could he exercise over her there? But even though he could not live with her, she was not getting another annulment. Never. She would continue as Richard's wife and keep him as comfortable as possible wherever he was. She twisted her little garnet ring. No matter what happened she was through with being single.

She watched as his shaking hand dipped the knife into the peanut butter. Making an adequate sandwich took

him at least forty strokes, but she forced herself not to
help.

The hungry dog waited patiently. Saliva began to drip
from his fanbeltlike gums. Richard set the sandwich on
the saucer. He and the dog exchanged a long, meaningful
look. As the dog's head drooped downward Richard slid
the saucer toward Cheryl. "Ladies first." He and the dog
watched in amazement as she began to cry.

"I'm just tired," she explained. That was only a half
truth. This sweetness of Richard's was making it harder
to send him away—like cuddling a baby intended for
adoption. She twisted the ring and reassured herself it
was not like that at all. She was staying married.

Chapter Thirteen

Rose hated the mandatory idleness of vacations. She took great pleasure in accomplishing things—in crossing out one activity after another on the back of a used envelope (laundry, vacuum, peel potatoes, do dishes). But in a motel room nothing needed doing.

And here at Cranberry Lake everything was damp. Beneath her back the mattress felt cold and moist. They were sleeping apart, too. The beds were narrow, but that was just an excuse. Al had cut her off. Beware of silent men, she thought. They judge, condemn, and punish without even the benefit of an argument. Maybe all that tranquillity surrounding them at home had been nearly this hostile and she had been too busy with her daily routine to notice. But she remembered the feel of his arms about her and knew there had been no hostility.

Her mattress was worn and slumped in the middle. She shifted her weight away from the caved-in section and lay stiffly on her side. Her restless movement had rearranged the sheets into a cloud formation.

She smoothed the wrinkled bed linen but gave up on trying to sleep. A dog barked. Another answered. And Rose smiled. God bless the North Country! If you were too agitated to sleep, it gave you all kinds of reasons for not doing so. Cocks began to crow at 4 A.M. and at 6 A.M. Fort Drum played reveille. After she had praised the proficiency and consistency of the musician, Al told her it was a record. That depressed her immensely, and this

97

morning when the canned music wafted in, she covered her exposed ear with the blanket.

Al stirred and got up. Later, when Rose heard the door quietly close behind him, she rolled onto her stomach and pounded her fists against the already defeated-looking feather pillow. How could he stop loving her like this? Why hadn't he refused to bring her here? Couldn't he have said he thought leaving Cheryl was wrong? But instead he had held his tongue and begun to hate her. What could she do? To challenge him would be like tackling an iceberg with her bare hands. She had no option but to square her shoulders and go on pretending she had acted correctly. And she collected change.

It would have been easy enough to go to a store or bank and request three dollars in quarters, nickels, and dimes. But that would have exhibited too much anxiety. She would call Cheryl when she had collected enough silver for the pay phone. What made it difficult was that Al paid for everything. She got back seventy-five cents by purchasing a map at a gas station. Then last night after he had taken care of the dinner check, she bought a roll of Life Savers for the fifty cents in change it brought her.

That had annoyed him. In his scheme of etiquette it made perfect sense to buy dinner for a woman you hated. "Why didn't you tell me you wanted mints?" he demanded.

She tore off the foil-end piece and extended the packet. "Want one?" She could see that he did, but he was too stubborn and pigheaded to accept one. The mints had become contaminated by her touch. But what had she done that was so wrong? It wasn't as if Richard had been a member of the family when he was taken sick. Cheryl had married him in that condition, and now that it was obvious she could not care for him, something had to be done. Al shouldn't be so righteous. He was the one who had opposed this marriage in the first place.

She dropped her arm. What she had thought were freckles now looked like age spots. Oh, God! What if this whole thing had nothing to do with Richard? It could be the age difference. Her whole body might have begun to repulse him. If so, then the hurt had to be hidden. If nothing else could be saved, she must at least salvage some pride.

She took deep breaths and began concentrating on her back. She again pretended it was composed of children's building blocks and mentally piled one block on top of another. The technique always worked. She immediately began to feel less stiff, and by the time Al returned, she was fairly calm.

He set a Styrofoam cup and an English muffin beside her. Then he emptied his pockets on the nightstand: a nail clipper, a small knife, and (at least) twelve quarters.

She coveted that money so much she dared not glance at it. "Going fishing today?" she asked casually.

"No."

There was a cheap little folding chair in front of their motel unit, and he took the morning paper out there. Rose decided he must truly hate the sight of her; it wasn't yet 8 A.M. and could only be about forty-five degrees outside.

As soon as the door slammed, she scooped up ten of the quarters and dumped them into her purse. Never before had she stooped so low. But once the money was in her possession she felt better. Revenge, she supposed.

If they left this damp, dreary motel, relations between them might improve. But they were trapped here because she had given the name and telephone number to Cheryl and Al's family. But when she called Cheryl today, she would explain that they were changing motels.

She had almost enough change for two calls. But she intended to stop worrying about change and just phone whenever she felt like it. Credit card calls were convenient. She would start calling every day. Was it too late in life to become an overprotective mother? Probably.

She took a couple of sips of coffee, then replaced the plastic lid. She didn't even glance at the muffin. It was probably dripping with butter. Besides, if he couldn't accept one of her mints, she wouldn't touch any food he offered.

Rose walked into the shower, quickly stepping over the mold in the grooves of the frame. She longed to clean this bathroom, but that would confirm her misery. Her present occupation was to pretend what Al was doing wasn't hurting her.

After toweling herself dry she dressed warmly in jeans, a turtleneck shirt, and the fisherman's sweater George had brought her from Ireland. She patted its thick weave. How could he have abandoned her to make such a fool of herself with a younger man? It occurred to her that she was becoming nearly as melodramatic as her daughter. She straightened her shoulders and stepped out onto the porch carrying her canvas bag. "I'm going for a walk."

"All right."

He didn't so much as flick an eyelash, let alone offer to accompany her. She had an enormous desire to hit him in the mouth with her soft yellow purse and scream, "If you can't act like a husband, then go away." But it was too late for abrupt, histrionic partings. They traveled in a shared vehicle with common finances.

Cheryl's first marriage had been an uncomplicated dissolution—property-wise. It couldn't have been so emotionally. Rose took a stone out of her clog and resumed her stride. Maybe she should have treated her child more tenderly. But she had always thought pampering and coddling canceled growth. Now she craved a little coddling herself. It was funny how rejection created a different perspective on the nature of independence. Well, there was still time to make amends with Cheryl.

She could see the Emerald Diner with its pay phone in the parking lot and began to run toward it. The glass door of the booth was cracked, the floor wet, but Rose didn't notice. She lined up all her money on the silver tray. The call only required $2.40. Six of Al's quarters could be returned to the dresser top.

The phone rang and rang, sounding as hollow and lonely as the cave she and Al had toured the day before. She replaced the receiver and tried to convince herself that worry was unnecessary. No need to be premature. Cheryl might have left Richard unattended while she went for groceries or the nurse's aide staying with Richard might be phone-shy. It was also possible that Cheryl was taking him back to the nursing home. The alternatives were too numerous to speculate.

Rose strolled back to the motel, kicking a stone in the direction of the topless bar she was required to pass. Though her first attempt had been thwarted, she was determined to become a gentler mother. Her own pain would be camouflaged completely. When Al left her, she would let her hair go gray and wear it in a formidable bun and look like a woman who has no use for a man.

Al had risen from his chair and was in deep conversation with the motel owner, a heavy woman whose deep blue sweatshirt matched her sneakers. The woman's hair was so short, it looked glued on. The effect was severe but made her look enormously capable. That's how I'll wear my hair, Rose decided.

As she watched the woman gestured urgently and patted Al's shoulder. That could only mean trouble. Somebody had called with bad news. When her clogs slipped off, she scooped them up and continued running. Richard must be dead. Cheryl might be under indictment. Al waited until the owner had returned to the office before he spoke. "My mother died."

His mother was the only member of his family he truly cared for. "Al, I'm sorry." She opened her arms to him, but he turned his back to her and walked inside.

Chapter Fourteen

Richard sat at the kitchen table and studied the red sandals Cheryl had just stepped out of. The imprints her toes had left were so distinct and deep that in moments of stress, he decided, she must curl her toes and press urgently downward.

Right now she was standing barefoot in front of the stove, stirring egg noodles with a wooden spoon. She looked pale, irritable. Perhaps, he mused, it was her tender time. But maybe she was bothered by the presence of the dog. She did not like Heinz and Richard didn't know if out of fear or jealousy; but just in case it was the latter, he never corrected her when she referred to Heinz as *he*.

Heinz was obviously a lady. You could tell by the delicate way she licked and groomed her feet. But Cheryl was responding to the appellation, which she assumed came from the German. How could she know the name came from the soup of fifty-seven varieties and indicated genealogy rather than gender?

Cheryl slammed the spoon on the counter, picked up a curved knife with a wooden handle, and began peeling an onion. When she turned to discard the skin, she had to fling it toward the garbage disposal because the furry expanse of Heinz prevented her from getting close to the sink. "Wherever you are," she told the dog, "it's in the way." *The bitch!* she thought. Yes, Heinz, peculiar name aside, *was* a bitch.

Heinz focused startled, injured eyes on Richard, as if demanding: why do we put up with this woman?

In response Richard looked up to the ceiling, down to the floor, and then toward Cheryl. *Her house.* He thought the dog understood for she crossed her feet daintily and raised her head in an elegant stance that seemed to proclaim: regardless of ownership, there is still only one lady on the premises.

Cheryl was watching them with a pouty left-out look. Richard knew she was far too busy examining her own hurt feelings to decipher his silent conversation with Heinz. But she did realize he loved the dog in a way he didn't love her. She should understand that the dog was all he had to show for his entire adult life. No small voices called him daddy. He wasn't even an uncle. But he had never known Cheryl to be especially perceptive and was sure she did not understand.

He looked at the indentations in her sandals again and couldn't help but feel sorry for her. He pointed to the dog and started to say, "I'm very grateful that you found—" Unable to finish, he swallowed and counted to ten; but he could still feel his eyes starting to tear. That was why he had avoided certain conversations. Expressing gratitude and reminiscing always caused him facial incontinence, which was, by far, the most humiliating type.

Cheryl, now given the upper hand, generously ignored his emotionalism and continued dropping huge chunks of yellow cheese into a saucepan. "Did you know," she asked softly, "that Jetlag Johnson has children?"

She must be following techniques suggested in those medical books he had seen her reading. *1. Change the subject and it will calm the patient. 2. Ask questions that require only one- or two-word responses.* Oh, hell, he might as well give in and let her be pleased with herself. "I knew they had one."

"What's his wife's name?"

Oh, God! He couldn't remember, so he decided to lie.

After all, Cheryl wasn't following the rules. She was supposed to be asking easy questions. "Joy." Richard beamed. That sounded right. In future instances of memory lapse, he would just lie and the right answer would automatically come to him. Further supporting details sprang to mind, one an anecdote he decided to share with Cheryl. "When they first started dating, I told him women named Joy were bound to be a disappointment. But he didn't listen."

"Joy Johnson." That someone had a name more lightweight than her own appeared to please her. She smiled and began clearing the table. That was when he remembered Jetlag's wife was named Linda.

Clearing the table was not a quick job, because its surface was covered with items necessary to his personal hygiene. When he was able to stand, washing in the bathroom did not require much. But to shave here at the table, he needed a fold-up mirror, a dishpan full of water, a washcloth, shaving cream, and a razor. Grooming his hair still only required a comb. But brushing his teeth had become an Olympic event. For every performance, she brought a toothbrush, the toothpaste, a Dixie cup full of mouthwash, a large glass of water, and the kidney-shaped bowl that patients everywhere were supposed to spit into.

When she started for the sink to empty the dishpan, he snapped his fingers at Heinz and commanded, "Out of the way." Heinz trotted into the living room with a haughty look. A few seconds later Richard and Cheryl heard *rip-tear-snap*. Heinz had torn down a section of the custom-made curtains by the sliding glass door. Richard hoped it was just a tiny bit of material from one drapery hook to the next. That much damage would indicate slightly hurt feelings, not deep anger. But Heinz had never been cooped up this much, and Richard didn't know what to expect from her.

Cheryl, tiring of striding back and forth from the kitchen to the bathroom, shoved the remaining articles to the table's side. "Your lunch is ready," she announced. "Pasta primavera."

His appetite was slowly returning, but he would have preferred canned macaroni and cheese with its pale, bland sauce to this colorful rich stuff. He ate a few noodles. "Have some with me."

"Too many calories." She walked into the living room and he heard her scream. "My curtains! Damn you, dog!" She must have lifted a newspaper, for Heinz scampered into the kitchen twitching nervously.

"Quick, Cheryl," he hollered, "take her outside." But it was too late. Heinz was already leaking on the linoleum.

"Get me a mop."

"Oh, Richard. You can't." Her flushed anger subsided. She stepped around the puddle and began pulling paper towels off the plastic roller. Each sheet of toweling contained a simple recipe for homemade salad dressing. "No permanent harm done." She became artificially pleasant and insincere, undoubtedly displaying the strained patience that the well-bred exhibit toward the sick and feebleminded.

The stupid cow. She was the one who had caused this mess by being jealous of a bewildered dog. "Get me a mop," he snarled in his best I-don't-like-to-ask-twice tone. He knew he was being cruel, but brusqueness was necessary. If he didn't display authority now, she would treat him like a patient forever.

Mopping, like bowling, was a matter of alignment. He edged his chair forward, following the vertical cracks of the linoleum as he mopped in front of him. When the lane was clean, he plunged the mop into the Lestoil-filled sink and started over. Turning around with the dripping mop was an awkward procedure that edged Cheryl right out of the kitchen, but he didn't care. The floor was getting cleaned, except for one persistent yellow stain near the table. When repeated rubbings did not erase it, he leaned forward to apply more pressure. His chair slid out from under him and for one dizzying second he was suspended in air, then fell downward with knees bent. From that vantage he could see the stain was candle wax and not of Heinz's doing.

The woman stood in the doorway staring. He noticed the full fringe on her cutoffs, the freckles on her knees, and her short, vulnerable-looking toes. Her feet advanced onto the wet floor and toward the telephone. "It'll be all right," she said breathlessly. "I'm going to call the rescue squad."

"No." The tender feelings he had developed toward her disappeared. Why did they need the rescue squad? The kitchen wasn't on fire.

"Put the chair tight behind me," he explained patiently, "then lock the brakes." He felt her pulling faintly underneath his armpits. "Don't pull. Just guide me." He got hold of the armrest and, by pushing with his foot, managed to heave himself into the chair. "Well, we made it," he told her cheerfully. He had been careful to keep all his weight off Cheryl.

She was unimpressed with his chivalry and good humor. "You son of a bitch," she screamed. "You've got this much strength, and you've been letting me tug on that Hoyer lift all week. Damn you."

He had never seen her like this. She was wild, absolutely wild. She stormed to the silver bread box, and he thought she might start hurling Pepperidge Farm rolls at him, but she dumped them on the counter instead. Then she carried the bulky box over to the table and flung his toothpaste and razor into it. "I'm tired of having your crap all over the kitchen table. When you've finished cleaning up, put your personal things in here."

She shoved his chair into the living room. He could see Heinz hiding under the bed, acting as she did during an electrical storm. Things were definitely out of control here. "Cheryl, honey, you're tired and hungry. Let's have some of your pasta and then take a nap."

They all went to bed. Heinz came out of her hiding

place and stretched out beside him. He patted her pretty paws, drummed his fingers on her head, and tickled her under the chin. She had a black mole on her chin with coarse black hairs sprouting out of it—her beauty mark. " 'You're so vain,' " he crooned, " 'you probably think this song is about you.' "

"A-a-ow-ow. A-a-ow-ow," she howled in chorus.

He put his finger to his lips. "Shh, Cheryl is sleeping."

Heinz looked back, lead-eyed. It was obvious the women did not care for each other.

Cheryl slept all afternoon, then staggered down to the couch and stretched lazily. "You were right. I was tired. I'm still tired. I don't even feel like cooking dinner."

"Don't."

"It's important that you eat regularly."

"Cook TV dinners."

"Too much salt."

"Too late to worry about it."

She shrugged. "All right. There are a couple in the freezer." But instead of heading toward the kitchen, she went and yanked down the gaping curtain, then flung it over the metallic lift. "We don't need to use this thing anymore? I just guide you?"

"That's right." He beamed at her approvingly. She was slow, but eventually she caught on.

She fixed his favorite TV dinner, the one with thin sheets of lasagna, green beans, fruit, and pudding. What pleased him even more was that she sat down and ate with him.

They were almost finished when the doorbell rang. Startled, they stared at each other for a second. The paper boy had already collected. Who else would be coming to their door?

It was Rose. Cheryl let her in with obvious reluctance. Richard watched in amazement. The generally impeccable Rose appeared thoroughly unkempt. Her hair was greasy. Her eyes were red. Even the laces on her yachting

sneakers were untied. "What happened?" Richard asked
bluntly.

"Al's mother died."

"I'm sorry," Cheryl said, and sat back down. There
were no additional chairs in the room, and Rose stood
there awkwardly. "Just wanted to see how you were.
And it looks as though you're doing fine." She fiddled
with her car keys nervously.

Richard pointed to the full coffeepot. "Have some coffee with us. There's a chair right inside there."

She peered at the chair in the dining room and hesitated, but when Cheryl handed her a coffee cup, she
walked meekly over to the stove with it.

When Rose's back was turned, Richard gave Cheryl a
warning look: *you are doing slightly better, but there's
room for improvement.* Cheryl stared back haughtily with
an expression she might have picked up from Heinz. He
gave her an even graver look. Finally she dragged a cush-
ioned chair from the dining room for her mother to sit
on.

Rose smiled at her gratefully. "Thank you, sweetheart."

"How was your trip?" Cheryl asked. Before her
mother could answer she carried her dinner tray toward
the sink and dumped it in the garbage pail.

Rose blushed. "I've interrupted your dinner."

"Oh, no. We were just having a snack of TV dinners.
All week I've been cooking big meals, so tonight we
decided to eat lightly. I told Richard these things have
too much salt in them for him, but he loves them."

He had to interrupt, or she would prattle on with this
nonsense all evening. "How was the trip?"

"The weather was kind of cold." Rose crossed her
arms as if she still might feel a chill. Then in a startling
revelation, she announced: "And Al and I had a tiff. A
serious one, I'm afraid."

"Want to stay here tonight?" He looked to Cheryl for

confirmation, but she was shredding their dinner napkins into the garbage pail.

Rose shook her head. "Oh, no, thanks. I've got lots to do at home. The funeral is the day after tomorrow."

Shortly after that she left. As soon as Cheryl heard the ignition, she banged a serving spoon into the metallic sink. "All week I've cooked nourishing meals," she wailed, "and she has to drop in the night we're having TV dinners. It's been like that all my life. She never sees me when I'm doing good. Though I don't know why I care, after the way she left us high and dry last week. They'd still be on vacation if it weren't for Al's mother. She didn't come back for us."

"I'd like to go to that funeral."

She smiled indulgently, as if he were a precious child fantasizing about some impossible feat. "I know you would."

He smiled back. He was damn well going to attend that funeral.

Chapter Fifteen

For most of his life Al had known he was stupid. His father helped him reach that conclusion at an early age. Sam Valerino skimmed his elder sons' report cards with absentminded approval. But when Al brought *his* report home, Sam put on his brown-framed glasses with the gold hinges and retreated to his reclining chair in the living room. On those occasions he rocked steadily, instead of leaning back and putting up his feet, as was his habit. His worn moccasins smacked against the green rug as he scrutinized the C— reports. He appeared to be searching for something, and Al always hovered near the reclining chair awaiting the explosion that never occurred.

The ten-year-old was just outside the door the night Sam said to Marie, "If only he was lazy or a discipline problem, there'd be some hope. But effort and deportment are always his best marks. You can't punish a kid for being naturally stupid." Sam should have known Al was in hearing distance. But maybe he didn't care. Delicacy was not his strong suit. Not that he was deliberately cruel. He had just never learned the fine art of tact.

Sam was an overworked clock repairman who was fascinated by Civil War memorabilia. He had once driven all day so he could photograph his three sons standing behind a pyramid of freshly painted cannonballs in Gettysburg, Pennsylvania.

Al's two brothers, Joe and Frank, shared their father's interest. At the dinner table they would lean back in their chairs, relaxed and expansive, to discuss General Lee's brilliance or Jefferson Davis's alleged pettiness. Over dessert the discussion switched from personalities to political theory. State sovereignty was always a favorite.

Al and his mother took no part in the conversation. Marie watched the table with the mien of a hash-house waitress. Did a water glass need refilling? Should the second pan of lasagna come out of the oven? During the analysis of the battle of Bunker Hill, she would thrust the ice cream back in the freezer and rinse the metal scoop.

Al was not vigilant like his mother. He just ate. Faster and faster and faster. Sometimes he clocked himself, as if dinner were a marathon he might conquer by speed. By ten he was a master at being otherwise engaged. If your mouth was full, he reasoned, no one would ask you a question and your fundamental ignorance could be hidden for one more day. At school he faked allergies and blew his nose constantly, certain that no teacher would interfere with this important bodily need. Some did. Then afraid to hazard an answer, he sat mute and ashamed until a more verbal student responded. Sometimes a teacher remained staring expectantly at him. That was the worst. "Don't you remember any of this, Albert?" Those teachers, Al was sure, would gleefully dismember dead birds. They had no mercy. So at dinner he shoved another clump of lasagna into his mouth and checked his watch.

"Don't stuff," Marie often reminded him.

He was never offended. She meant well and was the only one on his side. The night Sam proclaimed him stupid, Marie immediately disagreed. "His talents lie in other areas." She spoke firmly and not just to spare his feelings either. She sincerely believed he was a mechanical genius. All on account of the laundry room door.

For two years none of them could close that door. Sam pulled on it, then Joe and Frank tried jointly to slam it. When none of them had any success, they forgot it. Then one day Al got down on his hands and knees, ran his hand over the floorboard, and discovered that a giant nail had worked its way out of the wood. After he hammered it down, they were again able to shut the laundry sounds out of the kitchen.

Marie was more than pleased; she was ecstatic. Because of his simple carpentry, she considered him brilliant until her dying day.

Al's eyes started to tear again. He brushed the tears off his sore, swollen face and raised his arms straight out as if swimming on his back. He needed to reassure himself that he was in bed alone and able to cry openly. Then it came to him that Rose was gone, had left him. She had taken her beige luggage somewhere else. No matter. Don't waste time thinking about her. *She* was alive. He needed to remember Marie while her face and voice were fresh in his mind or else she would fade and be forgotten the way Sam had been.

Marie's hair had been coppery and she used to coil it on pink plastic rollers every Saturday night. She never went to parties unless she was the guest of honor. On those occasions she wore a gingery scent and a full-skirted electric blue dress. But mostly Al remembered her in white pedal pushers, washing vegetables at the sink, a big silver colander by her side.

Though never sickly, Marie had constantly monitored her health. When Sam had an outburst, she took her pulse. She believed a fever indicated the presence of cancer and kept a thermometer on her nightstand so she might discover the dread disease at an early stage.

Once after eating lunch, she had gone into the downstairs bathroom to brush her teeth and screamed, "I'm hemorrhaging." Al dashed in and stared at the sinkful of pinkish suds and saliva; he then gently reminded her that she had just eaten strawberry Jell-O. She patted his shoulder, letting him know she considered him both sensible and wise.

Since she was the only one who recognized his talents, he stayed in her presence as often as possible—drying dishes while she washed, dusting while she vacuumed. Sam wouldn't have tolerated such sissy behavior in Joe or Frank, but with Al it was different. He had no expectations for his youngest son.

At the onset of his teens Al himself began to wonder if he wasn't spending too much time with his mother. He was developing, but not in the right way, and he did not know what to do. He certainly couldn't tell Sam.

Sam took all troubles personally. If there was a noisy party in the neighborhood, he thought the ruckus was produced solely to disturb his sleep. When children trampled the edges of his garden in their running games, he mopped his brow and proclaimed, "They hate me. They all hate me." So if Al confided in him, Sam would immediately seek out a willing listener, glance dramatically skyward, and pronounce, "God is punishing me. My youngest son was born stupid, and now he's growing tits." Then Sam would mop his brow and grin mischievously. It was impossible to dislike him. Unless, of course, he was your father.

But Sam was dead and had been for fifteen years. Al forced himself out of bed and stumbled toward the shower. It was ironic, but in trying to preserve Marie's memory, *Sam* was becoming clearer and clearer. That had not been Al's intent at all. He switched on the shower head and soaped himself. His chest was broad, hairy, and appropriately masculine, but that had not been the case when he was thirteen.

He had worn loose T-shirts all the time to mask that he was about ready for a training bra. Finally he told Marie. She did not betray his confidence. When Sam demanded to know why she needed extra money, she did not tell him about Al's weekly hormone injections. Instead she backed up against the sink and proceeded to cry. In between sobs she sputtered, "It's just awful. It's just awful. I've worked hard all my life—just as hard as you. And I haven't got one cent to call my own. I have to account for every miserable penny."

It was a persuasive performance. For the rest of his life Sam left an extra twenty under the sugar bowl on Monday mornings and never asked how it was used.

The shots worked. The growth stopped. But what was already grown did not subside. Al began lifting weights. The additional muscles did the trick. Except that Al, in his father's and brothers' eyes, officially became a beast of burden.

At his father's request he mowed the lawn and painted the house. He took off the storm windows and carried down lawn furniture from the attic. He lugged the phonograph downstairs for his brothers' parties. Joe and Frank were close to finishing high school and in the winter they wore insignia jackets with washable white vinyl sleeves, which were a dull yellow by the time Al inherited one of them. It never quite accommodated his wrestler's shoulders.

Both his brothers were interested in girls. Joe, slim and doe-eyed, dated; but Frank, facially blemished and awkward, just watched. Neither felt any pressure. They were both going to college and convinced that the best still lay ahead.

Al, by the time he inherited a jacket, was himself attracting some female attention. One classmate in particular was drawn to him—a bleached blonde who wore pungent perfume and eye shadow the color of the sky in a child's paint-by-numbers picture. He didn't like her. The girls he fancied had shiny hair, well-scrubbed complexions, narrow feet—and no interest in him. Though he could not win these elegant girls' affection, he could get their attention—by scaring them.

He began following them home—not obviously and only partway. After a couple of blocks their narrow feet would start churning faster until they were practically running with their hair jiggling in a seemingly terrified way. Two of them even started walking together. He followed them both. No matter how fast they walked, he could keep a discreet ten paces behind without appearing to hurry. He was just out for a stroll. Nobody could accuse him of anything, aside from bearing a vaguely menacing air. He was big, swarthy, and lumbering. Apparently that was all it took to frighten those well-dressed squirrels.

It was the first time he had ever been considered a bully and that worried him—because he enjoyed it so much. While he was following the girls he felt on a high. But in the evening he would develop a crummy taste that no amount of mouthwash could erase. He never slept well on those nights either. He didn't discuss the situation with Marie because that was the year he began perceiving her as an innocent who needed to be protected from the seamier side of life. So it was just as well that Sam found him a part-time job.

He was to be an orderly at Deaconess Hospital. Marie didn't regard the post with favor. "If it's depressing," she advised, "just quit."

But Al loved the job. He especially loved hearing his name broadcast over the public address system. "Albert Valerino. Please come to the third-floor nurses' station. Albert Valerino. Please come to reception."

At any given moment someone in that vast hospital needed him. It was often an orthopedic case waiting for a push to rehab or an old person, frail as a wren, trapped on a commode. Being an orderly didn't require much talking either. All you had to do was push, lift, and take orders. Sam had given him a lot of experience in those areas.

One day a pretty nurse's aide remarked that he had the same forename as Albert Einstein. He sniggered and said, "Ain't that something. 'Cause I was born stupid." The aide just took him at his word and walked away.

Soon after he became an orderly he failed the Scholastic Aptitude Tests. The guidance counselor told him he hadn't failed; the tests were just an indicator. But she didn't advise him to apply to any colleges either, so he knew he failed.

He stayed on at Deaconess after high school graduation until he knew he was about to be drafted. Then he enlisted in the Marines. He chose the Marines, he supposed, in response to all the hype about the best and the brightest. At Parris Island, after Al and other inductees were shown a twenty-minute training film on brushing one's teeth, he knew he was not among the country's intellectual elite. (Both his brothers got deferments—they who loved to talk about war.)

Marie's cookies followed him everywhere, even to Vietnam. At his Quonset hut, they arrived in crumbs. He was a medic then and not crazy about his work. He hated the Huey pilots because they never looked back at the cargo of carnage he had to deal with. It was as if being college men exempted them from the messier misfortunes of war.

After Al was discharged Marie wanted him to interview with the large corporations that were moving to Connecticut. "No way," he told her. He did not want to spend his life working for college men. Her eyes watered when he said that. She knew he was never going to belong to a pension plan.

At first he just worked on building his house. He was still living at home when Sam had his heart attack. While Marie called the rescue squad, Al administered CPR. Sam was conscious and did not want to go to the hospital. "You have to," Marie told him.

That evening, just hours after Sam had died, Al and Marie sat at the big round table. They were waiting for Sam to appear, slam his fist on the table, point a pudgy accusing finger at them, and say, "I *told* you not to send me to the hospital. Now you've killed me. You hate me. You both hate me."

It was Marie who acknowledged their foolishness first. She got up for the whiskey bottle and poured two shots. "We'll drink to your father's safe passage."

Now Al lifted his coffee cup and drank to his mother's safe passage. Then he checked his hands and fingernails. They were as clean as a long soak in Clorox could get them. Marie always hated the state of his hands, especially lately when he had been doing so much logging and carpentry. She had wanted him to have an easier life.

Chapter Sixteen

Cheryl was dressed up for the first time since her wedding—nothing fancy, just a white eyelet blouse and a black skirt. But it was a flattering outfit. Because the skirt used to be skintight, Cheryl kept sliding her thumb under the waistband to confirm that it was a bit loose.

But her half-slip was not. It parasitically clung to her middle. So when she hooked her thumb under the skirt band, she also gave the elastic on the slip an outward tug.

Her behavior might have appeared odd had anyone been watching. But no one was.

Richard was forking up bits of broccoli quiche. It was pointless trying to get his attention while he was eating. He could only do one thing at a time. At home if she tried to talk to him while he was reading the nutritional information on the cereal package, he never answered. She didn't know if this single-mindedness was a result of brain damage or a heightened form of concentration left from his football career. Whatever the reason, the results were the same. She was at this postfuneral luncheon with no one to talk to.

Rose had been at the funeral Mass but had not come to the cemetery or the restaurant. Her earlier appearance made it all the harder for Al to account for her absence now. "An appointment," he told his brothers.

The flimsiness of the excuse didn't appear to worry either brother. They were talking stocks and bonds. Joe, the older, handsomer one, flashed a smile that included

117

them all. "Despite all these theories, investors are pretty primitive. Now that the weather is improving, the market will, too."

Frank, pale, with thick glasses, spoke exclusively to Joe. "That's too simplistic. The fluctuations have more to do with the deficit than the elements." Frank's wife regarded her husband intently, nodding occasionally in agreement.

Cheryl watched her. Elaine Valerino was the only other woman present. In earlier times Cheryl would have speculated on Joe's marital status; now, however, she concentrated solely on eating less than Elaine did. The woman was rail thin. She wore a simple black linen suit and white hose. No matter how shapely one's legs were, Cheryl thought, wearing white stockings to a funeral was showy and tacky.

Elaine shook the dressing off a piece of iceberg lettuce, then ate it. Cheryl sipped her tea and ate nothing. So far she was three bites behind Elaine. They were both having the chef salad, so gauging the woman's consumption wasn't difficult at all. Frank's wife shunned the unripe, yellowish cherry tomato but ate a piece of turkey.

Cheryl decided the long, stringy slice of fowl looked like fish bait and left it by the rejected tomato. She was now four bites behind Elaine.

It was an odd restaurant for Al to have chosen. A one-story edifice staffed by housewives who operated without a liquor license and served delicate low-calorie dishes. Today the room was empty, but it looked like a place frequented by women shoppers. Al must have come here once with Rose and remembered it was wheelchair-accessible.

Al was eating the fruit salad plate—and not pecking like he did at her house. No, he was eating the strawberries, the melon slices, and the clump of cottage cheese as if he were famished. The only accompaniment to Joe and Frank's stock market conversation was the constant click, click of Al's fork. Then he laid it down and ate a circular slice of orange. When everything else was gone, he began to pluck the grapes off their stems and eat them.

Cheryl watched his hands and noticed the thick tufts of hair above his knuckles. Gosh, she thought, even his hands are obscenely masculine. She was glad Richard didn't look that coarse. She was very proud of his appearance today. She had shopped long and hard for that navy sweater with its double buttons—a lot easier for him to get on and off than a suit.

But when she turned to give it another admiring glance, she noticed Richard had stopped eating. He was staring dreamily ahead and his forehead was shiny with perspiration.

He must be feeling dangerously weak. Well, it was his own fault. She had told him he wasn't physically capable of attending. But he had used his red phone to call Al and arrange for transportation. So she was trapped into coming with him.

Cheryl gave her skirt one more tug, then began to twist her wedding band. *Married, married, married*, it seemed to proclaim with every turn. Marriage had made her the stable one. She was forced to assume her mother's role. She gave the woman across from her a friendly smile and asked, "Is it much of a drive home for you?"

The blonde shook her straight, straight hair. "In good weather like this only about four hours."

Al's plate was empty now except for the barren grape stems. He stared downward. "Wasn't it just like Mom to wait for spring to die?" he asked. "She never wanted us traveling in bad weather."

There was an embarrassed silence and Al flushed—a painful reddening that started at the neck and slowly worked its way upward.

Richard, roused from his reverie, asked, "What was your father's name?"

"Sam."

"Wouldn't it be wonderful if she could drop you a note from heaven: *Having a wonderful time here with Sam*."

The blonde raised a delicate, braceleted hand to her face as if stifling a sneeze. Then she smiled and exchanged a long, meaningful glance with her husband that seemed to say: obviously crack-brained.

Cheryl wanted to slap her. Instead she plunged her fork into the cherry tomato and watched as the seeds and juice sprayed across the pale lettuce.

Chapter Seventeen

"You love that dog."

Richard nodded and continued eating his eggs. He knew that wasn't the response she wanted. What she wanted was for him to say something mushy. Something like "Oh, but I love you more." Forget it. He gave the dog to Al because Cheryl never walked her enough. Up where Al lived, Heinz could run free.

Cheryl slammed her hands into the pockets of her cutoff jeans and headed for the stairway. Had she stayed in the kitchen, he would have complimented her on her scrambled eggs. They were good—not dry, not runny, just right. But she had huffed off upstairs. He could hear the radio playing in her bedroom but wasn't able to identify the song.

Cheryl had an unfair advantage. She could go upstairs when she was disappointed in him. He had nowhere to retreat to get away from her.

At the moment that wasn't disturbing him much. Morning was his favorite time of day. Besides, the sun was out, and he was in excellent spirits. His stamina was improving. He rarely got nauseated nowadays. The night sweats didn't come as often. Additionally, he was regaining what his football coaches called "a positive mental attitude." Not only did he feel he could push himself through life, he almost felt sturdy enough to pull his wife along with him.

Richard shoved his plate away and glanced at the newspaper. He always read the want ads first. He wasn't sure why. Right now personal hygiene and getting dressed were a full-time occupation.

His reading completed, he pulled the bread box, which had become a fixture on the table, toward him. Toothpaste, a toothbrush, mouthwash, and soap were on the bottom shelf of the container. His shaving stuff was on the top. He reached up for his shaving cream and razor. Cheryl had left him a small dish of hot water, now lukewarm.

After the tedious ritual of shaving was accomplished, he took a sip of coffee. He ran his finger along the mug's handle and contemplated how much his life had improved. At the nursing home there was never any overlapping of function. He would never have been allowed to keep his coffee past breakfast.

Upstairs Cheryl was flipping from one station to another on her radio. What irony, Richard decided. If only she didn't demand it so emphatically, he might have been able to love her.

Richard shook his head. It was no good getting philosophical this early in the day. He had a lot of duties to perform. The challenge of getting in and out of Cheryl's tiny downstairs bathroom still lay ahead. Just thinking about it made him apprehensive. But there was nothing to do but get at it. He inspected his face one last time, then backed up the wheelchair and headed out into the hallway.

The blue-wallpapered bathroom was so tiny, the wheelchair would not fit in. So he was forced to leave it at the door, lean in, grab the sink, hoist himself up, hop in, pivot, and slowly sink down onto the cold john. When his skin touched porcelain, he thought *Whew, made it*, as if he had just accomplished something extraordinary.

There are times when you simply have to start over. He had not grown up knowing that. Rather, he had thought it was just up and up from apartment to condo to house to mansion. He had gotten as far as the condo when it all fell apart.

Getting out of the bathroom was even harder than getting in. Again he grabbed the sink, but this time he had to pull himself up and hop backward. Today, as always, he breathed a sigh of relief as he smacked against the vinyl of the wheelchair.

Richard surmised that he was fortunate in several ways. Cheryl always gave him privacy. If she started to come downstairs and noticed the empty wheelchair in the hallway, she would immediately retreat. Her kindness and consideration were genuinely appreciated. But, all in all, Heinz was better company. He found Cheryl so moody and inconsistent. Today at breakfast she said she wasn't hungry and didn't eat anything. Instead she kept eyeing an unopened package of chocolate mint cookies as if they were an adversary far stronger than she. And sure enough before she ran upstairs she grabbed the cookies. Right now she was probably devouring them two at a time, as out of control as a leaf on a windy day.

Richard maneuvered himself toward the living room. When he got to the stairs, he grabbed the banister and pulled himself up. Taking two steps was like trying to drive a car with one tire, but he forced himself to make the effort. He pulled a T-shirt out of the chest by his bed and pulled it on over his bedgown, easing the paralyzed arm in first. Then he dropped back on his bed and pulled on jeans. His morning work completed, he jerked his chair over by the patio door and watched a blue jay dive onto the patio. The jay's breast was a solid, elegant blue, but his tail was a mottled mix of blue, black, and white that reminded Richard of a loud polyester shirt Jetlag had once owned. All of a sudden he ached with loneliness. Seeking a remedy, he turned on the TV.

When Cheryl came downstairs, she had a crease running down the side of her face. It looked almost like a scar. Richard switched off the *Love Boat* rerun and gave her a kind smile. He wondered if she missed her friends from work. Maybe soon they could invite people over.

"Want to go outside?" she asked.

"Yeah."

She pointed to the patio.

"No. Out front." He liked it better out there, especially now that Al had built him a wooden ramp. Besides, there was more to watch.

He maneuvered himself into the sun, then waved at an elderly man carrying a sack of garbage to the Dempster Dumpster.

Cheryl remained standing on the sidewalk, squinting up at the sun. She looked lost. He pointed to the empty space beside him and said, "Get a chair and come sit with me."

"The sun isn't good for me." But she nonetheless went inside and returned carrying a folding lawn chair.

She stretched her pale legs out in front of her, stared at her aging green car, and sighed loudly. "I guess I'll have to find a mechanic. Can't very well expect Al to take care of it anymore."

"He'll still work on it."

She turned and gave him an accusing look. "Is that why you gave him the dog? To keep him in the family?"

Damn her! Would she never abandon the subject of the dog? He thought she would be so relieved to see Heinz obediently hop into Al's truck. He supposed the problem was that he had not consulted with her first. "Al's up there all by himself," he explained. "I have you."

That appeared to satisfy her. She nodded and changed the subject. "Next month I have to go back to work."

He didn't think that would be such a tragedy. He, at least, would get to see her in a dress again. Except for Mrs. Valerino's funeral, all she had worn for the last month were jeans or cutoffs and T-shirts. Though he had to admit, she was beginning to look better in them. Her contours were changing. She no longer resembled the little fat girl. She looked . . . He turned, gave her an appraising glance and the right word came to him. She looked *stacked*.

Cheryl, unsettled by his mystifying scrutiny, got up to

go inside. The chair had left wafflelike prints on the backs of her legs. "I'm going in to get us some books." She returned with a Regency romance for herself and a large-print mystery for him.

His vision was no longer impaired. He wasn't sure why she continued to bring him large-print books. But the big print did make every book look weighty and important. This skimpy whodunit was about the same size as *War and Peace*. Genre fiction had never really interested him, and he found himself reverting to the reading habits he had at fifteen, flipping through and only concentrating on sexy stuff. Mostly, though, he watched the passersby.

A wedding party drove past, honking their horns exuberantly. A piece of crepe paper came off the lead car, hung suspended in the air for a moment, then plopped on the ground, snakelike and abandoned.

Richard looked over at Cheryl. He wondered if she, too, was struck by the contrast between this boisterous wedding and her own. But she was totally absorbed in her book. He had scanned a couple of her romance novels, but even if he hadn't, he would have discerned pretty accurately how the protagonists acted. Following an afternoon of reading, Cheryl often took on the characteristics of one of the heroines.

She usually ended up with a strong desire to arrange flowers. Which wasn't easy, because she hadn't planted anything in the flower beds. When Rose lived here, he bet, the beds had been full of zinnias and pansies. Now all that bloomed were the rhododendron.

So Cheryl was forced to buy a prewrapped two-dollar arrangement at the grocery store. But that wasn't really inconvenient, because the people in her novel ate well, too. So Cheryl generally found herself shopping for groceries anyway. After she immersed herself in *Summer Rendezvous* or *Dangerous Partings*, though, the tinfoil-wrapped hamburger patties in the freezer quickly lost their appeal. Seafood or Cornish game hens and fruit-filled turnovers seemed more appropriate.

Tonight she came back with chicken breasts and two carnations wrapped in green paper. After plopping the baby's breath and carnations in a vase, she fixed cocktails, a British custom, though she and Richard both preferred wine.

Richard sipped at his martini and watched her ready the chicken for the oven. Her stay in the sun must have calmed her because she moved slowly and looked uncharacteristically content. Her legs, however, had turned a painful scarlet.

"You're really sunburnt."

She looked down, shrugged, and smiled.

"Doesn't it hurt?"

She poured dry vermouth on the chicken before answering. "No. I'm fine."

Richard decided that the cook's state of mind must directly influence the food. This was her best meal ever. The chicken was succulent. But what was exceptional was the lemon-mushroom sauce that accompanied it.

"With the sunburn and all, I feel like I'm on vacation on some island."

Cheryl, who never allowed herself to eat normal meals, got up for seconds.

Pleased to see her enjoying food, Richard reached over to touch her. But the phone rang and she leapt up for it, leaving him with his arm in midair.

"Oh, fine," she confirmed to the receiver. Then she stretched out the extra-long cord and walked into the living room.

Why can't she talk in the kitchen? Richard wondered. Though he couldn't see her, he could still hear her.

"Yeah, we'll be home. Okay, then. We'll see you around 8:30."

He hoped Al was bringing Heinz over, or that Rose

was finally letting them know where she was. But when Cheryl slammed the phone into the cradle and started to sob, he knew it wasn't Rose or Al. "He's bringing June here. To this house!"

"Who is?"

"Stu. They're bringing us a wedding present."

It sounded like a nice gesture. He couldn't understand why she was so upset.

She sniffed and stared down at her sunburnt legs, then voiced the real problem. "I look terrible—like a fat old lobster. I haven't got anything to serve them either. I only bought a package of two apple turnovers."

He tried to be patient, even if she had just handed him a heck of an insult. She never cared how she looked in front of him. Patience. Patience! When he gathered his self-control, he said, "I think there's a cake in the freezer. We can serve it with coffee."

"I don't remember any cake." She opened the freezer and pulled out a Pepperidge Farm chocolate cake and slammed it on the counter. "You're right." Then she frowned at the clock. "Are you all set here? I've got to wash my hair."

Cheryl not only washed her hair, she changed into a green and white dress so low-cut that when she leaned over he could see the tiny satin bow on her brassiere. It was prettier than what she had worn to their wedding. A pair of navy slacks and a white shirt were slung over her arm. "You better change."

"I'm all right."

"Please." She seemed on the brink of tears again.

To keep peace, he lay back on his bed and slowly pulled on the slacks. Was this tactless or what—asking him to go to all this trouble for her ex-husband? But he kept quiet about it. He didn't want a scene right before they were expecting company. They didn't get that much company.

* * *

The Freedmans came in jeans. Cheryl may have felt overdressed, because after ushering them in, she disappeared in the kitchen for a long time.

Stu set down a large, brightly wrapped package and gave Richard a professional handshake. "How are you? You're looking good."

His wife offered a sincere smile and a tiny hand, embellished only by a slim gold band. Brittly thin and slightly older than Stu, she radiated kindness. Her hair was long, full, and shoe-polish black. Strictly from a bottle, Richard mused. She picked a pillow off the couch and admired it. "Cheryl does crewelwork?"

"No. My mother-in-law. She lived here after her first husband died." Now she lived in a budget motel. He quickly got off the subject of Rose by fixing the Freedmans with a pleasant smile. "Do you work, June?" he asked.

She pushed herself back into the couch and nodded. "I'm a mental health nurse. That's how I met Stu. We both worked at the Highland Mental Health Center." Realizing she had embarked on a sensitive discussion, she flushed and began to fiddle with the fringe on the pillow, looking up once to give him a shy smile.

Her front teeth crossed, an indication she didn't come from money. She looked as if she didn't sleep well, maybe even roamed the house at night, wondering how much she had hurt another woman. Now she had come to make peace.

She couldn't know that it was impossible, that Cheryl collected and saved slights—*mean mother, dead father, no-future job, unfaithful husband*. Richard had heard it all when he was in the nursing home. If he were more dependent, she might try to add him to her list as *crippled husband*. But he wouldn't let that happen. No way. Marrying him was one of the few positive things she had ever done.

Though conversation was nearly nonexistent, Stu looked comfortable enough. He was the type who could make smoking seem like an all-engaging occupation. "What have you been up to, Stu?" Richard inquired. "You're looking fit."

"Feeling good. I've hooked my exercise bike up to a computer and now I get a reading of pulse, heart rate, and everything. I keep monthly printouts of my progress. Keeps you motivated."

"I bet." Richard wished Cheryl would haul her ass back in. How long could it take to make coffee?

Just as he considered calling her, she appeared carrying a tray of coffee mugs. She trudged back to the kitchen for the cake, then stood there flustered. Serving food already was rushing it. But as long as she had started, he tried to help. "Forks," he prompted.

"Ahh." Her shoulders sagged imperceptibly—except to Richard.

He watched her trudge back to the kitchen. Damn it, he wanted to scream after her, don't act defeated. There is absolutely nothing to be defeated about. You have the stronger husband.

When they finished eating the cake, Stu handed Cheryl the package. "Something June made for you."

She slit the tape, then slid off the wrapping paper with exaggerated care. Richard gave her an encouraging look. "Hurry up," he said mischievously. What he meant was: show a tiny bit of enthusiasm if you possibly can. He thought she tried. When she lifted the wicker basket filled with silk purple flowers, she exclaimed, "Oh, how pretty."

"Look underneath," June instructed.

Cheryl pulled out a handful of handmade place mats. Just as she was about to mumble something appreciative, June gazed at the rose-covered seats on their living room chairs and wailed, "They don't match. I should have called you about colors."

"We always eat in the kitchen," Richard bubbled. "They'll look great in there."

June's flowers proved to be indestructible. Right after

the Freedmans left, Cheryl hurled the basket against the refrigerator, but it landed handle-up with its cargo of spring blossoms undamaged.

"Why don't you put them away? Give them to your mother when she moves from the motel."

"I don't need your advice." Then she added, accusingly, "You didn't have to be so lovey-dovey to her."

"They were our guests. We were both polite."

She did not answer. Instead she began to gather the plates and saucers. She rinsed them and dropped them into the dishwasher as if she wanted to rid the house of all evidences of Stu and June's visit.

He watched her. When an appropriate moment came, he would try and comfort her.

Finally she noticed him. "I'm sorry," she said coldly. "You need help getting undressed. Don't you?"

"No hurry."

She dried her hands, walked into the living room, pulled the comforter off the bed, and tossed it onto the couch. "Ready?"

"Yeah."

She put her knee between his and hooked her right arm around him. They moved gracefully like a pair of figure skaters. Under her gentle guidance he stood and removed the shirt, then dropped onto the bed. But then she became another Vernice barking orders. "Lift up." He raised his arm when she handed him a bedgown and put his hand on her breast.

"Richard," she yelped. But she did not move away.

"Get yourself a gown."

"What?" Finally she understood. "I don't know. Maybe we should wait." She gave him an anxious look before going into the downstairs bathroom to change. He didn't know why she had to be so damn modest; they were married.

She appeared in the light blue gown. "Are you sure you're able?"

He ignored her. "Sit here, right beside me. You take off my gown and I'll take off yours."

She did as she was told. But her hands were clammy, and it took a while to get the sash of his gown undone. He had no trouble with hers. It was as easy as unveiling a painting. But God, what a lot of woman. No wonder she was moody. What an abundance of hormones it must have taken to create these mounds and valleys. As he moved his hand down her body, her chest turned a flaming scarlet as if it, too, had been sunburnt. She remained silent, except for once whispering, "Oh, Richard. Oh, Richard"—as if he had given her an expensive, unexpected present.

Chapter Eighteen

Al pulled the boy in the plaid Levi's shirt to the front of the bus. There were no empty spots, so he told a pony-tailed first-grader to move to the boy's vacated seat. She tightened her grasp on a Strawberry Shortcake lunch box but did not move. He gently tugged on her free arm, then escorted her three rows back.

"Sit," he commanded the boy. The kid slunk down, then pulled a wide-tooth comb from his pocket and proceeded to examine it. Damn him, Al thought. He could at least pretend to be scared. He gave the unobserving boy a stern look, then walked back to check on the boy who had been punched. The tubby, freckled victim was sitting hunched forward in the seat over the radiator with Al's handkerchief wrapped around his nose.

"You all right?"

"Yeah."

He knew better than to rely on what the boy said. Children always insisted they were all right. Several times, pale, quivering glassy-eyed kids had told him they were perfectly fine; moments later, they were puking into the aisle. Now he relied on his own instincts. He pulled the handkerchief away and examined the boy's nose. It did not look broken and the bleeding had stopped. He patted the kid's damp shoulder. "Sit back—and try to stay quiet," he advised.

Returning to his own seat, he noticed the bully's blue-plaid shirt was ripped on one shoulder. Had he done that when separating them? He hoped not. If he had, there

132

would be hell to pay. The brat's parents might sue. It was a crazy world. You weren't even supposed to help out at a car accident anymore because somebody you assisted might sue you later.

The little girl with the lunch pail generally gave him a shy wave after she left the bus. But today she marched in front of it without even a sideways glance. He just couldn't win with women anymore.

Even Richard's dog wasn't grateful. He always fed her as soon as he got home. But she never admitted to being hungry. She paid no attention as he spooned the canned food into the silver pie plate—though he knew she would gobble it up as soon as he went back in the house. Tonight he looked at Heinz's pale, proud head and said, "Don't act so offended. Your dinner is just as good as mine."

It was true. All he ever ate were TV dinners and canned food. In some mysterious way Rose had robbed him of his cooking ability. Before they were married he had been an accomplished, if uninspired, cook. But now even a scrambled egg was beyond him, so he bought cans of hash, beef stew, and pork and beans, and large-portion TV dinners. His nightly couple of beers had turned into a couple of six-packs or better. He blamed Rose for that, too.

She should not have deserted him. Women were supposed to hang around when you were giving them the silent treatment, find out why, then make it up to you. To pack up right after his mother's death had been unforgivable, but dragging him up to Cranberry Lake had been the worst thing she had ever done. Richard was his friend and needed him. His going away practically guaranteed that Richard would end up in a nursing home. The fact that everything was ending up differently didn't matter.

He ripped the tab off his third can of beer and dumped a can of hash into a Teflon frying pan. The composition *did* resemble the dog's dinner. He knew Heinz had finished her food by now. She just waited until he wasn't watching. To admit hunger would require gratitude. Heinz wasn't going to do that. She was sneaky—exactly the way Rose had been.

Rose never let him see her with wet hair or without makeup. Aside from some sex in the dark, he didn't know her any better than he had known his second-grade teacher. Once in a while he would see her rubbing her neck and taking aspirin. She must have had arthritis, but she never admitted it to him. Wasn't it the knowing of all those details that made a couple really married? Now when he caught a glimpse of her at school, he thought what a stranger she was.

She had given nothing. Instead she had robbed him of his cooking ability and made living alone unpleasant for him. He smelled the burning hash and ran to the stove. He noticed, as he plopped it onto a plate, that the bottom edge had turned black and crusty.

Heinz interrupted his meal by whining at the front door. He opened the door and she streaked by him. "Got too cold for you?" he asked, just to hear his own voice. He had lived alone for most of his adult life, but now it felt peculiar. He flipped on the TV on his way back to the kitchen. Lately he just about always had the TV or radio on—trying to kid himself into believing he wasn't alone.

He finished his hash, opened another beer, and thought about calling Rose. She ought to know the harm she had done. He stalked toward the phone, rehearsing what he would say. "You gave me nothing. You never let us be married. You . . ." He picked up the phone and dialed one digit. Then he remembered the few times he had attempted to discuss something important with her. She could never just listen. She always had to be doing something else—scrubbing the counter, flipping through the paper, or filling the teakettle. Nothing he could say was important enough to occupy her completely. Even if they started talking now, she would probably interrupt his train of thought and ask if she had any mail. He slammed the phone down. "Bitch," he hissed.

The phone rang shrilly. He jumped guiltily and his heart began to pound. She had heard him! He must have communicated through distance in a way that was never possible when living in the same house with her. He picked up the phone, ready to hear Rose say, "How dare you call me that!"

But the voice on the phone was pleasant, deep, and definitely masculine. "Hi! How are you?"

"Okay." It took him a moment to associate this strong, cheerful voice with Richard. Anticipating the purpose of the call, he said, "Heinz is a little homesick. But she's eating well. I built her a pen so she can be out when I'm gone."

"Good. How are *you* doing?"

"Okay." Al realized he was feeling his fourth beer. He was then doubly glad he hadn't phoned Rose. He would have stuttered and stammered and given her another reason to feel superior.

Richard became more specific. "What's happening there?"

He tried to think of something noteworthy and/or harmless but couldn't. "Nothing really. There was a fight on the bus. I guess I just wasn't quick enough. One of the kids got a bloody nose. And I'm afraid the other kid's parents will sue me for pulling him away."

"That's not likely."

"It could happen."

"If it does, we'll get you a good lawyer."

The *we* comforted Al. It sounded as if he had some powerful force backing him. He had an urge to tell someone how he felt: tired, drunk, scared, and dangerously angry. "I don't know, Rich, good buddy. Lately I've just been so pissed off I think I could really hurt somebody. Yesterday some woman pushed in front of me in the checkout line and for a second I thought I might haul off and belt her.''

"It's grief that makes you feel that way. You should get more sleep.''

"Na. I sleep all the time. All I do anymore is sleep, watch TV, and eat.'' Al blushed and silently cursed himself for saying such a stupid thing to Richard, who never left the house.

"That's good,'' Richard commiserated. "Sleep is very good for grief. It's healing. In the hospital I slept all the time.''

Of course, he was grieving. Hadn't he just lost a mother and a wife? Everything sounded so logical when Richard said it. He sometimes wondered if it was because Richard's statements were wise or merely because they were uttered with so much confidence.

As soon as they bade each other good night, Al stripped and got into bed. His friend had told him sleep was what he needed.

Chapter Nineteen

Cheryl sat in the back of the church. Going to Holy Communion was out of the question because she had not been to Mass since her wedding. But she was content to sit there and watch the people file by on their way to the altar.

Richard was spending the day with Al. They had left early, as if they had plans to go fishing or hunting. But she suspected they were just going to eat, drink beer, and play with the dog. And Richard would love it. Any variation in the daily routine pleased him.

He even enjoyed going to the mailbox. Yesterday he put the tiny key under his right thigh, then gave her a little wave as if he were off on a journey. Their box was four rows up in the metal structure, and Richard had to reach way up to fit the key in.

As he was pulling out the lone, white envelope, an elderly woman with rouged cheeks and a bright pink raincoat appeared. She pulled keys from her coat and gave Richard a flirtatious smile. "Don't they always give the highest mailboxes to the shortest people?" she asked.

Richard more than agreed. He nodded, flashed her his sweet smile, and said, "That's the truth."

My God! Cheryl thought. Her husband was six foot three. How could he have been so pleasant to that tiny woman?

Organ music, combined with untrained, quavering voices, always left her feeling raw and emotional. She gazed up at the altar and watched as a gray-haired woman in a belted raincoat exactly like her mother's received communion. When the woman turned, Cheryl realized it *was* her mother. Rose had let her hair go gray and had gotten it cut very short. But the effect wasn't severe. In fact, Cheryl had never seen her mother look so feminine and fragile. She continued staring, trying to decide what besides the hair was different. Rose, with head bowed, entered a side pew, five in front of Cheryl's. It was her posture, Cheryl decided, that had changed. Her ramrod straightness was gone. She wasn't stoop-shouldered, but she no longer had the look of a woman who knew exactly where she was going.

Cheryl flipped through her missalette. She read the aftercommunion prayers, but her concentration wasn't the greatest. *She should have called. She should have told me where she was staying. I shouldn't have learned it from Al.* Then she slammed the missalette shut. Always when she thought of her mother, it was because of some omission: *wasn't there. . . . Didn't love me enough.* At least in church, she ought to focus on something positive.

Cheryl and Rose smiled at each other, but out of reverence for their surroundings and because of the thunderous organ recital, they did not speak until they had passed the marble holy water fonts and were on the concrete steps outside. Then Cheryl gazed up at the sky, which had turned grayish black. "It was a dumb day to walk to church," she said.

"My car's down the street. Can I give you a lift?"

Cheryl followed her mother to the Buick sedan. As she was settling herself on the velour seat, Rose leaned over and kissed her cheek. It happened so quickly that by the time Cheryl turned, Rose was starting the car.

"How's Richard?"

"He's fine," Cheryl answered automatically. She didn't wish to get dragged into an exchange of pleasantries. Instead she wanted to think about that kiss. Last night her husband had loved her and now her mother was saying she loved her, too. It was too much to comprehend. She felt her eyes water up again. It was her day for feeling sentimental and acting sappy.

Rain began to pelt against the windshield. "Lucky I found you or I would have gotten drenched." Cheryl set her purse on the floor. The plastic car mats were immaculate—no pebbles, no dust, no sand. She bet one of the first things her mother had packed up when leaving Al was the cordless vacuum. She had such a phobia about dirt. Cheryl suddenly remembered her mother trying to scrub up oil and rust stains from the concrete driveway of their big house. No doubt it was George Farrell's Cadillac rather than visitors' cars that had leaked oil and rusted the driveway. It occurred to her that her father, who was always so neat at his office, used to create stains and clutter on purpose at home.

"You must be in a hurry to get back to Richard."

"No. He's not home." Cheryl paused, not sure if she should mention Al. But she decided she had no choice. Richard didn't have that many friends. "He's off with Al. That's why I don't have a car. Al borrowed it. It's too hard for Richard to get in and out of the truck."

Rose appeared to be only half listening. "If you don't have plans," she asked hesitantly, "would you like to go to the Dairy Bar with me for breakfast?"

Cheryl calculated how much money she had in her purse. She had cashed Richard's monthly Social Security check on Friday. There was money for something fancier than a diner or the Dairy Bar.

Rose took her silence for a refusal. "I bet you want to go home and just be by yourself for a while."

"No. No." Cheryl shook her head vigorously. She felt like celebrating. "Let's go to the Inn. My treat."

"That's pretty steep."

"I didn't do anything for Mother's Day. Let's make up for it today." She also wanted to make up for the impersonal, expensive guest soaps she had used as gifts for her mother over the last decade.

"Okay. I'm getting sick of the Dairy. Maybe it's the

low ceilings, but the people in there always sound as if they're screaming at one another.''

It was Cheryl's first visit to the Squantz Pond Inn, a favorite of New Yorkers. To her surprise the place seemed absolutely decrepit. She took her mother's arm as they climbed the rickety front steps. Inside the humped gleaming hardwood floors struck her as treacherous and she kept a tight hold on Rose. The gray hair didn't exactly make Rose look old, but it did give her a fragile quality. Rose had always been thin, but now she looked as if her bones might be made of glass.

Inside, a blackboard listed the brunch specials, though not the prices. The two women shed their raincoats and were led to a table in front of a nonfunctioning fireplace.

Rose fingered the peach tablecloth and glanced at the single white rose in the silver vase. ''Gosh,'' she said, ''this is posh.''

Cheryl regarded the Inn more as a mammoth firetrap. Had it not been raining she would have sought the fastest escape route.

Their Bloody Marys contained celery sticks that resembled ship masts. When Cheryl pulled hers out, it splattered the table with pinsize spots of red. Rose, she knew, would make a neater job of it. As she watched, Rose set the celery on her butter plate. Only then did she notice that her mother's nails lacked their customary bright polish. This caused Cheryl to feel a little panicky. What if Rose was thinking of entering a convent? The longer she considered this, the likelier it seemed. Why else would she leave her husband, quit using makeup, and move into a budget motel?

Rose took a gulp of Bloody Mary as if garnering strength. ''There's something I've been wanting to tell you.''

Cheryl's heart began to pound. She thought of visiting her mother in convent reception rooms with their stiff-backed uncomfortable chairs. Why now—just as we're beginning to understand each other? Besides, she thought self-pityingly, her taking the veil will leave me an orphan.

"Now that I know how it feels, I wish I had been more supportive when things didn't work out between you and Stu."

"Aw, him." Cheryl waved her hand in a dismissing gesture. Stu was the last thing she wanted to discuss. He was ancient history. "Besides, you weren't left, Mom. You left Al."

"Only because I had to. He didn't want me anymore. He wants a younger woman."

Cheryl shook her head in bewilderment. There was nothing the least bit youthful about Al. The blue polyester slacks he had been wearing this morning reminded her of a Florida retiree. And lately he had developed the beaten demeanor of a man who thought his life was over. "Are you sure? Did he actually say that?"

"There were signs."

"I don't know. Al's not acting very happy alone. When he went for his bus driver's physical, his blood pressure was very high. Richard told me. He and Al are buddies, you know. They've gotten in the habit of talking on the phone just about every night. Richard is pretty worried about him."

Al's welfare clearly wasn't a topic Rose was comfortable with. Her eyes wandered around the room, then rested on Cheryl. "You look wonderful. You've lost weight."

"A little bit. We're really eating healthy and when we had the dog I got into the habit of taking walks. My clothes are all big. I'll have to buy a few outfits before I go back to work."

Work! It was a subject Cheryl eradicated from her mind as much as possible—not because she dreaded the monotonous office routine but because of Richard. She had thought about it and decided it was just too long to leave him alone. If he fell out of his chair in the morning, he'd lie there all day. Her only alternative was to send him to an adult day-care facility. She knew what those places were like—dazed, weary old people in party hats. Hardly a party for Richard, though, and she was dreading telling him.

Cheryl set the rumpled peach napkin on the table and paid the bill.

"Thank you," Rose said, shy as a kid on a first date. "I'm going to look at an apartment now. Want to come?"

The apartment had a private entrance at the back of a two-story home. But it was a tiny studio, still occupied by an apparently very sloppy college student. Dirty dishes covered the counter. The kitchen cabinets were painted a garish pink.

Cheryl expected her mother to give it a perfunctory glance, then politely tell the owner it wasn't what she needed. Instead Rose agreed on a July 1 occupancy and left a deposit.

Cheryl was stunned. How could her fastidious mother agree to live in such a cramped dump? Unless she was short of money. Of course, that was it. When she had given up her condo, she had intended to live rent-free with Al forever. On the way out Cheryl said, "Let's go to the motel and get your stuff. I want you to stay with us until you move."

Rose shook her head firmly. "No! That's something you'd better discuss with Richard."

Cheryl nudged her toward the car and said equally firmly, "He'd love having you." This was one time when she knew she was going to win.

Chapter Twenty

Rose left the bedroom door open. Cheryl would be coming upstairs soon. Perhaps she would want to venture in and talk. Even though she was exhausted, Rose remained sitting in the upholstered chair, still wearing her floral ankle-length robe.

She heard her daughter closing the house for the night. The kitchen window was slammed shut. Both front door locks were clicked in place. Then the sliding glass leading to the patio squeaked closed.

Rose straightened and stared at the two-year-old magazine in her lap. She remembered the articles because it was from the stack she had left behind. Though she wasn't planning a trip, she reread an article advising women how to travel safely alone. When her daughter came upstairs, she wanted to look approachable. For too many years she had tried to avoid Cheryl's confidences. They had struck her as petty and self-pitying. Now circumstances had changed. Cheryl truly lived in a difficult situation and Rose wanted to comfort her.

After she listened to her daughter's problems there was some advice she wanted to volunteer. Sure, Richard had his limitations. But he wouldn't ever be unfaithful. Rose didn't know if Cheryl was aware of her father's infidelities. Just in case she wasn't, Rose would carefully sidestep the issue now. Still, her daughter should know that most married women are afraid. They are careful not to anger their husbands too much. With Richard, Cheryl would never have to experience the shame of a fearful retreat.

The downstairs lights blinked off. Cheryl wasn't coming upstairs! She was spending the night with her husband. There weren't going to be any whispered confidences between mother and daughter. It was too late for that. Cheryl had become a married woman in the traditional sense—loyal, courageous, and silent. Rose heard what might be a prelude to lovemaking and rushed to close her door.

Since leaving Al, she felt as if she had become a voyeur in other people's lives. From her motel room she had heard slamming car doors, raised voices, laughter—and none of it had anything to do with her.

In the morning she stayed in bed long after she heard activity downstairs. She did not want to witness Cheryl administering to Richard. But when she strolled into the kitchen no administering was going on. Richard was at the table reading the newspaper. Cheryl was nowhere in sight.

When he spotted her, he pointed to the half-full coffeepot. "Morning. How did you sleep?"

Rose poured coffee into the dainty china cup that had been set out for her. "Very well," she replied. She was half-afraid to face him. She had slept poorly and felt her face showed it. Richard could be very observant.

But he wasn't studying her. He was fixing raisin toast. "Want cinnamon sprinkled on your toast?"

"Sounds delicious."

"Here it is."

Rose walked over by the toaster. Richard had toasted and buttered the bread but was unable to bring it to her. The commendable thing about Richard was that he told you what to do. There was none of this uncertainty— should I or shouldn't I help?—that Rose felt around other handicapped people. She sat at the edge of the table. "What's going on in the world?"

"Nothing good. Want part of the paper?"

"No, thanks. I don't have much time. I have to be at school by 8:45." She was immediately sorry she hadn't taken a section of the newspaper. She could have used it to hide behind; for Richard had begun studying her with an intensity she found unnerving.

He was probably taking in her serious gray suit and lack of makeup and jewelry. She had even forgone wearing nice underwear. Instead of buying expensive, padded bras, she now chose stiff, nameless brands with cups that came to an obvious point. And when her silky underpants wore out, she replaced them with stiff, bandleg briefs bought at discount stores. Though her financial situation wasn't great, she wasn't changing her appearance to save money. It was more significant than that. She was doing it as a form of penance. She was letting the world know she was renouncing men. She wasn't young and should never have married Al, especially since her motivation was primarily physical. But she was putting all that behind her now. "Where's Cheryl?"

"Out digging up the front garden. The crazy woman is still in her bathrobe." He shook his head.

He had, Rose thought, a cute way of acknowledging Cheryl's shortcomings without criticizing or asking for sympathy.

Cheryl burst in and, without even a good morning, asked abruptly, "Is it too late to plant out front?"

"No. It's never good to plant before Memorial Day." Rose took another sip of coffee and glanced at her watch.

"Can we go for flowers this morning?" Cheryl asked.

"Honey, I'd love to but I have to go to work."

Cheryl put a grimy hand to her cheek. "Work. I forgot people did things like that. We're in our own little world here." Her eyes watered and she crossed her arms.

"Could we go on Saturday?"

"Yeah. Okay." Cheryl bobbed her head up and down the way she had as a teenager. "We'll shop and go out to lunch."

"Lunch will be my treat." Rose set her dishes on the

counter, then pulled car keys from her purse. Even with
a grown child, Rose realized, going off to work could
make a mother feel guilty.

Though she had looked forward to their outing all
week, on Saturday Rose stuck to her resolve of dressing
simply. Over her old ladies' underwear, she pulled on
navy slacks and a V-necked cotton blouse. The blouse
was cut a little lower than she now preferred, but she
couldn't possibly afford to buy a completely new ward-
robe.

Cheryl kept parading through the bathroom that ad-
joined the two upstairs bedrooms, modeling outfits that
were now too large for her. She stepped in front of the
big vanity mirror. "This is just huge," she proclaimed
proudly, twirling around in a black dress. "I couldn't
possibly wear it to work."

The waist on the dress did gap. Rose inspected it. "I
could make a tuck." Cheryl's face clouded. "But you do
need to buy some new things," Rose added quickly.

Cheryl regarded her mother's uniformlike outfit and
then reappeared with a long red-checked scarf. "This
will give you some color."

Rose took the scarf, tucked it under her collar, then
looped the front strands into a bow. The flashy scarf not
only made a sharp contrast with the rest of her outfit, it
pulled her neckline even lower. But rather than offend
her daughter, Rose accepted the scarf as an accessory.
She also put on lipstick and added hoop earrings.

"Where do you want to go for lunch?"

Rose shrugged. "Will Richard mind us being away so
long?"

"Na." He's going out with . . . with Al this morning.
And this afternoon he'll probably sleep."

Cheryl always mentioned Al with such reluctance.
Rose would have liked to tell her: *He didn't break my
heart, I just made a fool out of myself. I'm glad he and
Richard are friends. At least, something positive came*

out of our marriage. But it was too soon to say those things. She and Cheryl had not advanced to confidences. More time was required.

Rose did not respond to either of Cheryl's statements. She already knew Richard took an afternoon nap and thought it was quite wise of him. In fact, it probably saved his marriage. He woke up cheerful at a time when Cheryl was most prone to being testy. His nap also permitted them to enjoy their evenings, and they enjoyed their evenings more than Rose had ever thought possible.

She plopped her car keys onto the kitchen table. "I'll leave the Buick keys here for Al. He's more used to driving it."

"Thanks," Cheryl mumbled, relieved at not having to mention her stepfather's name again. "Let's go, then."

There was a sloppily painted sign on the nursery's porch: TWO HANGING BASKETS FOR THE PRICE OF ONE. Cheryl, never able to resist a bargain, bought four hanging plants for the back patio. For the front she selected petunias, pansies, and one salmon-colored geranium. In the checkout line she fingered the petals of the pink and white petunia. "It sort of reminds you of one of those crank record players."

"A gramophone?"

"Yeah."

Rose assumed Cheryl would drop the flowers at home and give them some water. Instead she immediately headed for the Interstate. "Let's go to the mall. Downtown is so dismal."

Rose nearly said: "The flowers need to be watered first." But she decided against it. She vowed not to do or say anything that might exhibit disapproval, at least not until her relationship with her daughter was firmer. A tough pledge. It wasn't yet 10 A.M. and already her head ached and her neck was stiff. She used to practice breathing and mental exercises that helped alleviate tension but had given them up. When stress became constant, no exercise could combat it.

She wasn't a shopper. It would have been impossible for her to approach a crammed rack and scoop out the one dress that would be perfect for her daughter. Still she knew what would be all wrong. She watched Cheryl approaching the dressing room with a slinky red knit that wouldn't have been flattering on a beanpole.

Rather than interfere, she wandered from the dress department and began to look for a water fountain. If the department store had one, perhaps she could find a plastic bag and transport some water out to those poor, half-dehydrated flowers.

There was no water fountain, but when she returned to the women's department, Cheryl had selected a silky turquoise two-piece outfit that was very pretty and quite expensive.

"That's very smart," Rose assured her. "Get one quality outfit, instead of a lot of things that won't last." That had not been Cheryl's intent at all and Rose knew it. But she desperately wanted to get those flowers watered.

Cheryl sighed and gazed down at her parcel. "Yeah. That's what I decided. Want to eat lunch here?"

The restaurant was four floors up and hidden behind the housewares department. Cheryl immediately ordered them both whiskey sours, then said defensively, "I need a drink. I have to go look at that day-care center this afternoon."

Rose poked at her cherry with the swizzle stick. There was a skylight and the hanging plants surrounding it reminded her of the flowers still trapped in the trunk. They are just objects, not people, she reminded herself. She couldn't remember precisely when she started being so concerned about plants, animals, and possessions, but it happened shortly after her first marriage. Probably George's affairs had made her realize possessions were more permanent than people. So she had become a gardener and her housekeeping even extended to scrubbing the driveway on blazing hot afternoons.

But Cheryl was her daughter and certainly more deserving of her attention than some drooping plants. "Is this day-care center well run?"

"I doubt it. But it can't be as repugnant as that nursing home."

Rose smiled nervously. *She* could offer to look after Richard this summer. She had planned to enroll in a course in teaching the developmentally disabled, but staying with Richard would be more pleasant. They could talk, read, watch television, and—Rose speared the cherry savagely. And she would inevitably become too involved in her daughter's marriage. Besides, when fall came, he would still have to attend the day-care center.

Cheryl dropped Rose off at the house before going to inspect the facility. But she didn't want to take the time to unload the flowers. "They'll be all right," she assured her mother.

"It will only take a second. Let me carry them inside."

"Okay." Cheryl reluctantly pulled the keys out of the ignition and handed them to Rose.

Rose pulled the flowers out of the trunk and placed them on the sidewalk. She then returned the keys to Cheryl. The Vega restarted with a high whining sound.

Poor kid, Rose thought as she watched her daughter drive away. Still she was relieved she hadn't been invited to come along.

She entered the house quietly. From the hallway she could see Richard asleep in bed. When she turned toward the kitchen, she had to stifle a scream.

There was a man's arm on the kitchen table. Her heart missed a full beat and then began pounding wildly. She forced herself through the doorway. "Hello," she said as calmly as she could manage.

Al continued drinking beer from a can, one of the low-calorie brands Cheryl kept in the refrigerator. He had left her car keys in the middle of the table.

To anyone else she would have said, "Oh, you startled me." But it was foolish to admit shortcomings to a man who had rejected you. She was very conscious of how awful she must look without makeup. *I don't dress for him*, she scolded herself.

They had nothing to say to each other. Besides, Richard's sleeping pretty much prohibited conversation. Rose grabbed Cheryl's small orange watering can from the counter and took it to the sink. It seemed to take forever to fill it up.

Rather than reentering the house, she used the outdoor faucet to refill the watering can. Once the flowers were watered, she lined them up in orderly arcs in front of each bed, changing the arrangement twice.

When she could stall no longer, she went back inside. Al was still sitting at the kitchen table, but the beer was gone. She gave him a stiff smile, intending to say "We really appreciate your befriending Richard" with all the formality she could muster. But she was afraid her voice would falter and he would know how much he had hurt her. Al had spent much of their week at Cranberry Lake without speaking. She shouldn't let a few awkward moments force her into starting a conversation. Besides, he would be forced to depart sometime.

There was a large coffee stain on the counter. As she took the dishcloth off the sink faucet, she heard his chair scrape backward. Thank God, she thought, he's finally leaving. She began scrubbing at the stain. When he grabbed her left arm, she dropped the dishcloth. Her right arm automatically shot up to her glasses. The frames were wire and got bent easily. But he did not strike her. "Let go of me."

He pressed his chin down onto her shoulder and hissed softly, "Upstairs."

It was like a dream. She tried to scream and couldn't.

Her legs wouldn't move. He pushed her forward. On the bottom step he lifted her and began to carry her upstairs.

For a crazy half second she leaned her head against his chest for comfort. When she jerked it away, she could see Richard's sleeping form through the stair rails and was glad she hadn't been capable of screaming. It would have frightened Richard, who, moreover, could scarcely help her.

Al dumped her on her own bed and she silently repeated over and over: *I won't scream. I won't scream.* That was as close as she could come to praying.

He knotted Cheryl's scarf around her wrists, unbuttoned her blouse, then yanked her poorly fitting bra upward.

She kept her eyes closed and didn't struggle. There was no point. *Just let him do it and get it over with. Life would go on.* She even lifted herself up so he could get her slacks off easier.

She did not open her eyes until she heard him leave by the front door.

Chapter Twenty-one

Richard hoped no one else was outdoors. Such raw grief should not be witnessed. He was watching Cheryl through the screen door. It was much like a funeral ceremony. First she would lift a plant, turn, then slowly plod toward the Dempster Dumpster. Now she was dropping a box of pink petunias into the green garbage receptacle.

He would like to get her back inside. But there were three boxes and one hanging plant left. She would not stop until all evidence of that shopping trip with her mother was erased.

He had hidden her new dress under his bed. If she saw it, she would destroy it and then be sorry later. Rose's note, the cause of all this grief, still lay on the table. It had been hastily scrawled but was still legible: *Must get away by myself for a while. Thanks for everything. Rose*

If only he had woken before she'd left, maybe he could have talked her out of going. But damn it, she should have known better. For the first time in their lives, she and Cheryl were getting close. Rose's departure had wrecked it all.

When Cheryl came back in, he would try to get her to take some aspirin. Maybe that would help her calm down. But he didn't want to issue an order. It would be better if he could just hand her a couple of tablets and gently coax her into taking them.

Getting his hand on the little plastic bottle of aspirin was the problem. Cheryl kept it on the bottom shelf of

the cupboard under the bathroom sink. He wheeled over
to the bathroom, reached in, and swung the cabinet door
open. There they were in the left corner of the bottom
shelf. She couldn't have put them in a more inaccessible
spot if she had tried.

He backed out of the bathroom and plucked a hanger
from the coat closet. By bending the hanger, he was able
to form a long-handled hook. But after a three-inch lift
the aspirin slid off and hit the blue bathroom rug. Finally
he just dragged the bottle into the hallway and ultimately,
the kitchen. When he leaned over to pick it up, he was
glad to find it did not have a childproof cap.

Cheryl almost took them. She even got herself a glass
of water. But then she shook her head. "Better not," she
insisted. The tablets he had worked so diligently to get
were set back down on the table.

Her face was pink and swollen from crying. She had
been chewing her bottom lip, and beads of blood had
formed on it. He had to comfort her somehow. "What
about a weak drink?"

She did not appear to hear him. "Was it my fault? Did
I do something terrible?"

"No."

"How could she?"

"I don't know." Richard had never held his own
mother in much esteem. But Rose was different: a shy,
strong woman who gave rather than took. But her behavior today didn't seem very generous. He couldn't explain
it at all. The most constructive remedy was to forget
about her for the time being. He crumpled Rose's note
and dumped it into the wastebasket. "How about a
drink?"

"All right."

He made her a weak manhattan. If he were a different
man, he could take her someplace suitable for dinner and
maybe get her to forget her troubles. Still, if he were a
different man, he never would have gotten involved with
her in the first place. He asked himself how he would

have regarded Cheryl if he had met her before his stroke. He wasn't proud of his answer.

She was staring vacantly in front of her.

"Why don't you lie down for a while?"

She looked at her watch. "It's almost dinnertime."

"We'll eat late."

He was relieved when she started upstairs. It could have been worse. Rose told him Cheryl had taken scissors and cut up all her clothes after her father had died. Then she had jaggedly cut off her own bangs, so short that neither barrettes nor scarves could hide the damage.

Richard decided, since he couldn't take her out to dinner, he could, at least, prepare a meal. Fixing supper did not require gourmet wizardry. His grandmother had not been much of a cook and her dinners had always been special. He tried to remember why. In the chest where Grandma kept her tablecloths there was a drawer full of seasonal trimmings. A small leprechaun with sturdy green plastic feet stood in the middle of the table on St. Patrick's Day. A crepe-paper and cardboard turkey, held together by a paper clip, occupied the same place on Thanksgiving. She had stickers, too. They were put on the dinner napkins—yellow ducks for Easter and red hearts for Valentine's Day. But the Florida heat dried out the glue, and as soon as the napkins were unfolded, the sticker always fell to the floor. But there was still cranberry juice in a real wineglass and the thrill of being treated like an interesting dinner companion. That was it! Having Grandma's undivided attention had made everything special.

Cheryl always had *his* undivided attention. He had made it his occupation to gauge her moods and bolster her shaky ego. So a memorable dinner was going to require something else—maybe a tablecloth and candles.

It wasn't going to be elaborate food; all the refrigerator contained was a head of unwashed lettuce, an unopened bottle of red wine, and a package of ground beef. However, there was a banana cake in the freezer, which he set out to defrost. He debated over what to do with the ground beef, then decided a meat loaf was classier than hamburgers. Besides, he had eaten a hamburger for lunch.

He and Al had gone to a root beer stand at noon because Al claimed not to be able to cook anymore. Richard thought that might be the truth because there was no evidence of anything but drinking going on at Al's house. He even had to pick up their morning coffee at a convenience store because he had even run out of Taster's Choice. Al's home was well stocked with beer, though. Cases of it were piled by the refrigerator, waiting for space inside.

It had been an awkward visit. Heinz stayed close to Al, occasionally nuzzling against his leg. That had embarrassed him. Twice he said, "She's never done this before." The second time he added, "Generally, she has no use for me." Both times he tentatively petted her, acting as if she might jerk away at any moment.

But she did not jerk away. Heinz, the rejected woman, might merely have been putting up a good front with the new master. But if she was not yet attached to Al, Richard knew she would soon become so. Heinz was a realist and knew there was no sense living in the past. Being a realist himself, he wasn't hurt by her coolness. The part of his life she had belonged to was over.

At lunchtime they got into Rose's car and drove to the big mall on Route 7. Between the Hickory Farm Store and Sears, there was a root beer stand that Al praised for its good hamburgers.

It was a narrow little place with the counter in the back and the tables in front. Al wheeled Richard through the entryway. Only a delicate wrought-iron fence separated them from the diners. Richard glanced to his right and stared directly into the face of an impoverished-looking old man eating french fries. The creases around the man's mouth fluttered as he chewed. Next Richard focused on the dark roots of a blonde whose thick makeup couldn't conceal intense disappointment. He had to look away. It was awful to be so intimate with strangers. In his infrequent outings he generally stared at belt buckles or blouse buttons and found the view more comfortable. How had he handled the pain in strangers' faces when he walked erect? He supposed he had never seen it. Back then he had been pretty wrapped up in himself and his career.

Al parked him at a table and went up to the counter. Richard saw him flinch as the uniformed girl bellowed their orders into a microphone. Poor Al's nerves were shot. Richard had known the guy was in trouble ever since Mrs. Valerino's funeral. He had even considered suggesting counseling. But it would offend Al and probably cost about eighty smackers an hour. Besides, he remembered what a wimp Stuart had turned out to be. He figured he could do just as good a job himself. In consequence, he called Al often and tried to get him to talk. But he never got very far. Al might tell him what was bothering him but never why. Maybe he didn't know. He wasn't a very reflective guy.

Al plunked down the tray that held their hamburgers and drinks and proceeded to eat in total silence. Purely for conversation Richard asked, "Glad the school year is over?"

Al shrugged, removed the pickle from his hamburger, then tossed it into the Styrofoam container. "Think I might stop driving altogether."

"How come?"

"Too many women drivers."

Richard did not understand how that affected Al. He was alone in his bus with the children and rarely came into contact with other drivers. Then he hit upon a reasonable explanation. "Do they bring down the pay scale?"

"Na." Al blushed and appeared unable to explain the matter further. They both reverted to eating their overcooked, tasteless hamburgers.

Tonight's meat loaf looked far more appetizing. Richard had opened the oven door and could see the meat juices turning a golden brown. The baked potatoes looked nearly done, too.

He dried the lettuce and fixed salads. Then he located a corkscrew, planted the wine bottle between his thighs, and pulled out the cork. Removing corks was always his job. Cheryl always jabbed the corkscrew in crooked and broke the cork.

Everything was ready except for the table. All he could find in the living room bureau were the violet place mats June had given Cheryl and the laminated used greeting-cards ones she had been given as a wedding gift at the nursing home. Using June's gift was out of the question, so he pulled out the garish ones from the nursing home. By candlelight they may not look too bad. The lemon candle was the stocky air-freshener variety set in canning jars. But its gentle light made the kitchen table look festive.

Cheryl appeared at just the right moment, wrapped in a terrycloth robe and mumbling ''I'll fix something fast.'' Then she took in the salads, wine, and oven smells. ''You fixed dinner. My God, Richard, everything smells wonderful. I guess I'd better go get dressed.''

He knew better than to expect her to get dressed up. In a few minutes she would wander back downstairs in a T-shirt and jeans or, at best, a worn wrap skirt.

Since their wedding she had only dolled herself up once and that had been for her ex-husband. He wished just once she would wear something new for him.

But she didn't. The black jumpsuit she reappeared in had been bought four years earlier in an impulsive moment and never worn because it was so low-cut in front. Richard took in the plunging neckline and the leopard scarf that belted her waist. But what he liked best was the way she had combed all her thick red hair over one shoulder. She was shyly waiting for his reaction. There was nothing to do but give a long, lecherous whistle. He was sorry for that unkindness he had entertained earlier about never giving her a second thought in his healthier days. If she'd been dressed like this, he would have noticed her. No question at all.

Chapter Twenty-two

C heryl stared into her mirror and repeated, "Dumpy, dumpy, dumpy." The new turquoise outfit she had considered so flattering in the store now pulled on her waist and made her feel sausagelike. She had so wanted to impress Derrigo and Raymond with her recent weight loss, but these separates did not convey thinness. Still, what difference did it make? Neither of her bosses had ever really noticed her before. Today wouldn't be any different.

Cheryl pushed her feet into white heels and started downstairs. She had to hold on to the banister because it had been months since she had worn anything but flats or sandals.

Richard had perked coffee and was preparing to make cinnamon toast. She was glad to be working only half days this first week. It gave her a little time before she had to broach the subject of the day-care center. Not that it was going to get any easier. Richard was trying hard to become proficient at cooking so he could be independent. That just made his staying alone all the more dangerous. She had grown anxiety-ridden. What if he spilled hot coffee on himself or if his clothes caught fire? It was just too dangerous for him to be alone. If Rose could drop in once in a while, it might be different. But Rose couldn't be depended on for anything. Cheryl ripped her toast in two, quartered it, then set it back on her plate. She had no appetite.

Richard noted her shaking hands. "The big-business lady is nervous," he said teasingly.

"I'm not nervous and I'm not a big business lady." She had not meant to snap at him, but any reference to successful businesswomen made her feel defensive. Richard did not realize how far she was from a briefcase-carrying woman executive. Those well-dressed professionals were always getting profiled in the magazines. Besides a great job, they always had a husband, two children, and curvaceous figures. Their constant publication of those success stories was one of the reasons she had canceled her subscriptions to several women's magazines. She far preferred reading romances. The characters in them never made you feel professionally inadequate.

She sipped the last of her coffee. "I better get going." Already she missed the leisurely mornings she and Richard were accustomed to and wished he would look a little depressed about her leaving. But as she pulled the keys out of her purse, he gave her an upbeat grin, the thumbs-up signal, and said, "Go get that bacon."

It was stupid to expect sympathy from Richard. With his rah-rah football background, he would view even her dead-end job as an opportunity.

Her watch was fast. The radio announcer said it was only 7:30. She still kept driving toward the Interstate. It might be good to get into the office early and get a feeling for what had been going on.

Lucy wasn't gone! Cheryl had assumed the office temporary's assignment would end the preceding Friday, but the girl's possessions were all over Cheryl's desk. An ivy plant sat on the ledge. A purple satin star-shaped pillow hung from a gold thread taped to the overhead desk light. On the desk itself a former soup can with an orange yarn covering held Lucy's abundant supply of felt-tip pens.

Thank God we didn't hire her at Christmastime, Cheryl thought. She would have brought in blinking lights and a life-size Santa. She stomped over to the adjoining desk, but it now had a coffee maker on it. There was also a supply of Styrofoam cups, a jar of Cremora, and large tray of sugar packets.

Was brewing coffee now part of the morning routine or something Lucy did on the sly? Cheryl figured it had to be the latter. Wasn't it Derrigo who always said he didn't want the office turned into a kitchen?

She stood staring at the pot, unsure of what to do.

"You're an early bird."

She whipped around and gave Derrigo an eager smile, which he did not return. He looked grave and older, but maybe it was just his brown suit. She had always thought the wearing of winter colors in summer aged people.

After switching on his office lights he walked over to her. "I'm glad you're here early. Why don't you make us both some coffee and come into my office?"

Cheryl carried the pot to the water fountain and blinked back tears. She took his command as a personal defeat. It had taken her years to train him to walk down to the first-floor coffee machine himself. Now she was going to have to start all over again. Besides that, he didn't look all that happy to see her back.

She added a lot of cream and one plump sugar to his coffee, then set it in front of him.

"That's great. Want to close the door, hon?"

What was going on here? Cheryl obediently closed the door, then sat tentatively in the visitor's chair—a space she had occupied only when taking shorthand.

"How is it going at home?"

Cheryl slid back in the chair and crossed her legs. It was all right. Nothing was going on here. Derrigo wanted to ask her about her husband's condition and was considerate enough to hold the conversation privately. "Things are going better than I ever expected," she told him honestly.

"You're looking refreshed."

"Thank you." She felt he had noticed her weight loss and was mentioning it in a tactful way.

He pulled a folder out of a desk file and placed it on his desk to indicate that the conversation was taking a business turn. He opened the folder but did not look at its contents. "You've been doing an excellent job for us for four years. I thought it might be the right time to offer you a chance for promotion."

Cheryl uncrossed her legs and kept her hands primly in her lap.

"There's a trainee course opening up next month for computer programmers. Several promising nonprofessionals have been selected to attend. And since you're extremely logical and a whiz with numbers, I thought it might be a good opportunity for you to break into the field. *And* into a higher pay scale." He raised his hand to prevent her from speaking. "No need to give me an answer now. I know it's something you'll want to discuss with your husband."

He picked up his pipe and rubbed his thumb against the wood of the mouthpiece. "There's another situation I think you should be aware of. We've hired Lucy full-time. Not because of any unparalleled office skills. It was more of a humane situation. Her mother—er—acquired a new boyfriend and asked Lucy to leave the house. To get an apartment, she needed to be working permanently."

Cheryl's hands were shaking, but she spoke calmly. "When I was offered a leave of absence, I was told my job or an equivalent job would be held for me."

"And it has been," he answered impatiently. "You can have your old job back, if you want. I could use you both. But this other opportunity is certainly worth considering."

"Yes, certainly," she answered coldly.

After thanking him perfunctorily, she stood and returned to the desk that held the coffeepot. Computer programmer? What made him think that was what she wanted to do? Be reasonable, she told herself. It has nothing to do with you. He just wants to keep Lucy on, and you're in the way. And Lucy, the conniving bitch—how convenient of her to get kicked out of the house right then. Well, she wasn't going into that trainee course. Why make it easy for them? Let him try and convince his management that he needed two secretaries.

She checked her watch. Lucy was fifteen minutes late.

Before a phone could start ringing, Cheryl grabbed the straps of her purse and walked down to the ladies' room. She went into a stall, pulled down her panty hose, and stared at her white unstained panties. Her period was three weeks late and showed no evidence of coming. Stress! She knew it was just stress. But this weekend she had even been afraid to take the aspirin Richard offered her. And she certainly couldn't take the job that Derrigo mentioned. She was going to have to fight for what was hers. As soon as Lucy made an appearance, she would force her to switch desks.

Lucy arrived, bearing a pink, brown, and white box. "I'm sorry I'm late," she hollered in to Mr. Derrigo, then, displaying the box of doughnuts, said, "I thought we'd celebrate Cheryl's return."

Cheryl refused a glazed doughnut with a curt "I'm dieting."

"Really?" Lucy acted amazed. "You look like you've lost a lot of weight."

Cheryl wasn't taken in by her. Anybody who dressed like Lucy couldn't speak the truth. The girl had on skin-tight black slacks, a white sleeveless blouse with a frilly yoke that dipped low in the back, and stiletto heels. The summer sun had bronzed her, and to highlight her tan, she had taken to wearing gold glitter eyeshadow and a peach shade of makeup.

While she was in Derrigo's office tempting him with a doughnut, a phone started ringing. Cheryl pushed in the call button.

"I'll get it," Lucy trilled, and with three quick strides

she was out of Derrigo's office, leaning over the ledge, and taking a message with one of her purple felt-tips.

Cheryl had nothing to do. She poured herself a cup of coffee. It would make her jittery. But she had every right to be jittery. Her job was in jeopardy.

Martha Austin appeared at Lucy's desk to welcome Cheryl back. She took a doughnut and listened to Lucy prattle about her weekend.

"He came over for dinner on Saturday night," Lucy said, keeping her voice none too low. Derrigo could easily hear her. If she was discussing boyfriends at the office, that must mean that she and Derrigo weren't having an affair. He had to be keeping Lucy on for some other reason. But Cheryl didn't have a clue as to what it could be.

"But the whole time he was over, all he did was watch my bed. I know it's a studio and you can see my bed from everywhere, but he could have been more subtle about it. I don't know—I just keep meeting the wrong kind of guy."

Maybe it's the way you dress, Cheryl hypothesized, as she silently drank her coffee.

"Was it like this when you were dating?"

"I've been married a long while," Martha answered complacently.

Less than a year, and you pounded lots of pavement before you found that guy. God, I'm getting vicious, Cheryl decided. I have to do some work. But what? Raymond's phone rang and she grabbed it, only to find she had to ask Lucy where he was.

"Belgium. He'll be back next Tuesday."

Cheryl was relieved to be on the premises for only half the day. She contemplated calling Richard, but it was too early. She didn't want him to know how desperate she was feeling. When Martha disappeared, she asked Lucy, "Do you have anything I could do?" She expected to be handed a month's worth of filing.

Lucy shuffled through the folders on her desk. "Most

of it's the yucky stuff I've been putting off—Xeroxing, filing.'' Then brightening, she said, ''Oh! Raymond left a tape. Want to do that? He's not crazy for my typing.''

Cheryl put her hand out for the recorder and miniature Dictaphone tape, but Lucy was staring through the desk divider at the coffee maker. ''Oh, gosh,'' she wailed. ''You've got all that coffee stuff on your desk. I'll get a typing table to put it on.''

''It's all right,'' Cheryl assured her, but Lucy was already racing to the supply room.

Cheryl checked her watch and decided it might be an ideal time to phone Richard. He didn't answer until the fifth ring and as soon as she heard his deep *hello*, Derrigo began to bellow ''Lucy, Lucy!''

''Richard, I'm sorry. I've got to go.''

''It's okay.''

She didn't know how it could possibly be okay. Doubtless he had gotten to the phone with no little effort. But don't let him get down on me, too, she silently prayed. I couldn't take that right now.

Derrigo dumped a load of legal agreements into her arms. ''This has got to go out to the Coast right away.'' He didn't appear to notice she wasn't Lucy.

After she sent the papers Air Express, she began typing Raymond's dictation. A speech he was outlining: ''You may well ask how the determination to acquire Majestic Corporation was made. And that's a valid question. At 107 million dollars, Majestic is the second largest acquisition in Software International's history.''

Derrigo's gray head appeared at her ledge. She removed the headphones and switched off the tape.

''Have lunch plans?''

''Not really.'' She had intended to go home and eat with Richard. But Derrigo had never invited her for lunch before, not even on Secretary's Day.

''Twelve o'clock okay? I drove in today.''

''I'll follow you, 'cause I'm going home after.''

''It's a date.''

Her face flushed. It was stupid to be flattered by his attention. He just viewed her as a convenient tool. But she knew that and was still flattered. I have no convictions, she thought. I can't even maintain a grudge. When Lucy gave her a shy smile, she smiled back.

"Thanks for doing that tape."

"I like typing." She cursed herself for being so pleasant. Her mother would have known how to freeze out this hussy. But she didn't even have the courage to demand her own desk back. "Are you going to be here for a few minutes?"

Lucy wrinkled her brow as if fielding a difficult question. "Yeah," she finally replied.

"I want to call my husband."

"Oh. I can disappear."

"No. I'd rather you be here in case Mr. Derrigo needs something. I don't want to hang up. My husband is in a wheelchair and it's hard for him to get to the phone."

"Boy, when you two said in sickness and in health, you really meant it."

More like mutual desperation, Cheryl wanted to say. That's what brought Richard and her together. And mutual effort would keep them together.

Richard answered on the first ring this time.

"Sitting by the phone?"

"Sort of. I'm baking a cake."

She could visualize all the dangers of the oven. And there was his walking now, too. He would start at the stairwell, take ten lurching steps forward, then hop back into the wheelchair. He was determined to walk again. But he could fall so easily. Maybe lunching with Derrigo wasn't such a good idea. "Mr. Derrigo invited me to lunch. But I don't have to go."

"No! Go!" He sounded anxious to get back to his baking. There was no point in prolonging the conversation. "Be careful."

He was enjoying his newfound privacy. There was no

doubt of that. If only she could afford to work part-time, maybe that day-care center could be avoided. But part-time workers didn't get any company benefits like insurance. She had to remain a full-time employee.

When she pulled into the parking lot at O'Hara's Café, Derrigo was pacing back and forth beside his Mercedes. He was also jingling the change in his pockets, the way he did before meetings with his superiors. He was nervous! That observation calmed her, and she took her time getting out of the car.

O'Hara's was dimly lighted and well air-conditioned. Cheryl felt as if she had just entered an underground cave. Because she had difficulty seeing, Derrigo, a regular patron, led her to a table by an unlit fireplace. His behavior was puzzling. He wasn't treating her like a date, but he wasn't treating her like a secretary either. It wasn't until they were through with their appetizers and he had ordered her a second drink that she figured it out. He was treating her like an equal—like another man.

"How did Stu feel about your coming back to work?"

It was blasphemous to let him refer to Richard by that name, but too dangerous to correct him. She was going to have to stick to a neutral *he*.

"Happy, I think. Even when I was home all the time, he liked me to get dressed up and go out. Then he liked me to come home with stories about what I did and saw. When he unpacks the groceries I buy, he even likes to hear about the supermarket."

"That's good. When Marge first went back to the nine-to-five world, I wasn't very pleased. She talked about her job all the time. She wasn't making all that much money, so I didn't know why it was so important to us. But now I realize how important it is to her."

She watched his stubby fingers fiddle with the unlit pipe. "And I'm beginning to enjoy doing some of the cooking—making my own breakfast, stuff like that."

Welcome to the twentieth century, Cheryl thought as she nodded enthusiastically. "My husband enjoys cooking, too.'' The drink was inducing euphoria, a calming state similar to the one she experienced after her monthly cramps ceased.

''It doesn't sound like Stu would stand in your way if this job is something you want.''

''Oh, no,'' she answered proudly. ''He never would. He's a big believer in figuring out what you want and going after it.''

''Then, is there anything to discuss?''

She knew he was manipulating her. But she thought about carrying an expensive briefcase and wearing well-tailored suits. The biggest plus would be having her own phone—one without call buttons. ''I guess not. I guess I want to enroll in that class. Would I have my own office?''

''As soon as you pass the course, you'll have your own office in the Applications Development Department. Sound good?''

She nodded like a happy child.

''In the month that's left I hope you can help Lucy get up to speed. She's a good kid, just a little rough around the edges.''

The coffee sobered Cheryl and her head began to ache. She had let him do it again. For the price of one lunch, he had gotten her off his payroll and into A.D.D. expenses. The man was no fool.

As she watched him fix his coffee with cream and two sugars, a comforting thought occurred to her. One more month and I'll never have to fix his coffee again.

Chapter Twenty-three

"I hate you." Richard only said it once. To have repeated the statement would have implied that he was out of control and hysterical. He was not, though Cheryl would probably have been gratified if he were.

"You don't mean that," she said calmly. "You're upset."

He stared at her coldly, and she backed into the corner by the silverware drawer. She was dressed for the first day of her class in a blue suit she had bought over the weekend. He had coaxed her into buying it. Then he had spent the rest of his weekend trying to build up her confidence. "If you want this badly enough, you can do it. You aren't too old or too slow a learner. At least give it a chance." And now with a few well-chosen words he intended to tear her to shreds.

"This is a fine time to tell me. Isn't it? Now that a wheelchair service is coming in a few minutes. Day-care! You decided—no discussion, no nothing. You think you're so important. The only reason you're in this class is because your boss wanted to get rid of you. You fat, cowardly—"

She slapped his cheek. The resulting crack unnerved her. She leaned against the counter and began to sob.

He wasn't moved, had no desire to comfort her, and was glad when the doorbell rang. Unfortunately the wheelchair service attendant backed him out of the house, so he had to continue staring at her.

"He'll be okay," the attendant told her cheerfully. "They always are, once they get there."

There were three old people in the back of the van. He couldn't see their faces, but he supposed their circumstances were similar to his own. Marriages were over, friends were gone. . . .

He had an opportunity to put an official end to the marriage right after he got to the West Side Center. A capable-looking woman in purple slacks and a coordinating tunic top shook his hand. "I'm Kay," she said kindly, "and I'm sorry I didn't get to come to your house and meet you. But we've been so busy with people going on vacation and sending their parents here. You are a little younger than most of our guests."

Kay bent down and peered into his face. She was blonde, fairly young, and her perfume smelled like pine needles. "You're getting a black eye." She pushed him through the living room and into a cubicle-size kitchen. After giving him some ice, she asked, "How did it happen?" When he did not answer, she added, "Don't be afraid to tell me. If someone is abusing you, there are things that can be done without jeopardizing your safety."

It would be so easy. But he wanted Cheryl to be the one to end it legally. Let her call the lawyer, get the annulment, and find a place to send him. She was the one who had wrecked their marriage with her sneakiness. He shook his head firmly. "I am jus-s-t clum-ssy." He spoke haltingly, as if making the sounds were difficult. He didn't need her prying into his life right now.

The guests started their day at the West Side Center with warm-up exercises. The eight residents made a circle and bounced a multicolored beach ball to one another. He noticed that most of his companions wore sweaters. The center could have saved itself some money by turning off the air conditioner.

The ball only came Richard's way once, and he obediently swatted it away. He saw no point in being hostile.

The only other male, an old guy in a gray cardigan,

wasn't participating at all. He paid no attention to the ball, just constantly mopped his eyes and blew his nose. As soon as the game was over, the man backed his wheelchair over by a window and Richard followed him.

The women moved to a long folding table where various Christmas crafts projects were in progress. A blue-jeaned aide approached him, probably to bring him over to that table, but Kay called her away.

Richard was grateful. He liked this spot. The sun was warm and he felt relieved that the glassy-eyed old man wouldn't talk to him.

He wondered if Cheryl had gotten herself to the programming class. She had once told him that in all her years as a secretary she had never sat down in any of the men's offices. What she did when talking was perch in the doorway, and if a professional came along, she immediately left even if in midsentence. Nobody should live like that. He hoped she was safely in her class.

This was the cruelest part. Though she had betrayed him by springing this day-care stuff, he was going to think about her—wherever he ended up. He was going to have to learn to live with his infirmity—and without Cheryl.

Kay came over to Richard's neighbor, placed a hand on his forehead, and proclaimed, "Mr. McGrath, you're a little feverish." She quickly wheeled his chair away. The spot where he had been sitting was marked by a half circle of used Kleenex. When no one was looking, Richard grabbed one of the discarded tissues and pressed it to his mouth.

Chapter Twenty-four

Al hoped the pastor was hearing confessions. The confessional box was thickly curtained and fairly sound-proof, so there was no way of finding out ahead. Once in there, it was too late.

What would he do if it was that young priest? He broke out in a cold sweat just thinking about it. That guy would want to have a conversation afterward. *How old are you? Working? Do you get out much with people? What made you feel bad enough to do such a thing?*

He couldn't stand that. The only way he could confess was to kneel in front of St. Theresa's old pastor. You could mumble your sins to Monsignor Tarisi, then high-tail it without fear that he'd try to get personal.

If only there was someone he could ask. A heavy woman in a shapeless black dress was at the end of the line of prospective confessors. She wore dark stockings and sensible, lace-up shoes. Her steel-gray hair had been forced into an untidy bun. He used to think this somber-ness was an Italian custom. But he had come to believe it was something more fundamental than just custom—something in the genes.

After Rose left him, he began to shun all his favorite checked shirts, and now wore only solid brown, a bad choice for summer since it made any underarm wetness spectacularly apparent. But Al didn't worry about his appearance anymore. He supposed this old woman didn't care either. He looked back at her again and then knew what he was going to do. Once she left the confessional, he was going to wait a few respectful minutes, then approach and ask who was hearing.

If she said Rosselli, he would leave. If it was Tarisi, he would bow his head and get in line.

He was going to have to wait awhile, for there were still three people in front of her. Having a plan calmed him. He sat back in the pew and began to rehearse what he would tell the monsignor. "Bless me, Father. My last confession was about two years ago." (It was two years exactly. He had gone right before marrying Rose.) "These are my sins: I've missed Mass, drunk too much, and in June I raped my wife."

He had thought adding the month and attaching the word *wife* made the sin sound less grievous. But just imagining saying it made his stomach queasy. He wasn't going to be able to go through with this. He stared at the gold squares in the ceiling above the altar and wished he could push back the clock thirty years. Back then he had liked coming here to Saturday morning confession with his mother. He had loved the ornate ceiling and the gold chandeliers with their red glass. But he had never been allowed to come to Sunday Mass at St. Theresa's. Sam felt churches named after women were inferior; so the Valerinos always went to nine o'clock mass at St. Virgil's, where the priests were unfriendly and there wasn't much parking.

Monsignor Tarisi came out of the vestry, made his way in obvious pain around the altar, then limped down the three marble steps leading to the middle aisle. The janitor, carrying two folded chairs, met him there. The monsignor sat on one chair and rested his injured foot on the other. The janitor reappeared carrying a portable confessional. It had a burgundy kneeler and a window with a black curtain as thin as a nun's veil.

Al decided he might as well leave. Only the pure of heart could approach such openness. He stood, then began to rush up the aisle toward the confessional as if his very survival depended on it.

He just couldn't live with this burden anymore. It wasn't because he was afraid of missing out on heaven. He didn't expect that much—just a place like a dentist's waiting room where the saved spent eternity reading back issues of *Newsweek*. He had to confess and be forgiven because he couldn't breathe. Forcing himself on Rose left him suffocated. If he didn't soon get more oxygen, he would die.

The monsignor's injured leg appeared to hang suspended from the confessional's side. His black knit sock and priestly loafer made an innocent picture. How could Al trespass on it? He didn't know. He just had to do it.

"Bless me, Father." He spoke low and thrust his head forward so his nose brushed against the curtain. ". . . and in June I raped my wife." He said it so quickly the words all blurred together.

"Why?"

Al's heart leapt in fright. There weren't supposed to be questions, especially out in the open like this. He gulped and repeated, parrotlike, "Why?" He forced himself to remember that day in the kitchen. Rose had been scrubbing on a counter stain. "I was hurting and she wouldn't pay any attention. She acted as if cleaning or watering the flowers were more important than me." His voice broke pitifully.

The monsignor appeared to understand that he had become too weak for extended speech. He asked simple questions. "Have you forgiven her?"

"Yes." Al wanted to leave so badly he would have agreed to anything.

"Do you want to harm her again?"

"No."

"I want you to call Catholic Family Services and make an appointment with the counselor. Now make a good act of contrition for your penance and say three decades of the rosary."

"Oh, my God, I am heartily sorry for my sins because I, I . . ." He couldn't remember. He had been praying it all his life and now he couldn't remember. The father gently prompted him, and somehow he was able to finish.

"I absolve you from your sins in the name of the Father, Son, and Holy Spirit."

Al was forgiven but he didn't feel any better. He felt hot and sweaty, as if the fires of hell weren't burning all that far away. His head still ached as if it were acutely oxygen-starved.

He had expected immediate relief. After all, it was a valid confession. He said his penance in the cab of his truck, counting out the decades on his fingers and adding five extra Hail Marys just to be sure. He had remorse for his sins. He had been sorry immediately for hurting Rose.

She had been so meek and compliant. He had thought it meant she still loved him. Then he had run downstairs and seen Richard sleeping. She had not struggled or cried out because she didn't want to frighten Richard. While he, who was supposed to be Richard's best friend, had totally forgotten about him or had been too drunk to care.

Now Richard was lost to him forever.

He switched on the ignition and headed toward Main Street. "It doesn't matter," he told himself. "I wasn't a real friend. I was a convenience." He tried to convince himself that Richard had used him as a beast of burden the same way his brothers had. But the memory of Richard at his mother's funeral kept interfering. He could remember Richard sitting in the restaurant. Pale, his eyes glazed. He had been too weak to come and had come anyway. There was no denying what his friendship had been. It was a big loss.

Al turned off Main and headed toward Constitution Square. He had never been one to ask for favors because he hated getting turned down. He still remembered the humiliation of asking his first-grade teacher if he could be excused and having her say "No. Go back to your seat" loud enough for the whole class to hear. Being refused had shamed him more than wetting himself.

However, in this one particular instance, he didn't have much to lose. He would ask Cheryl if he could visit Richard. If she turned him down, which she undoubtedly would, he was no worse off than he was already.

No. That wasn't quite true. If she was truly frightened of him and thought he had come to harm her, she might call the police. He did have something to lose.

Later on he admitted to himself that he never would have stopped at their condominium. Two brave acts in a row were more than he was capable of. But he saw the blinking lights of the rescue squad from the street, so he jerked in and parked by Cheryl's Vega.

He sat there too stunned to move while they brought Richard out on a stretcher. He was getting oxygen, but Al could tell from the leisurely pace of the medics that it was far from a life-and-death situation. The ambulance also left at a reasonable speed without the siren.

In haste everyone had gone off and left the condo's screen door wide open. Since there was nothing else he could do, he ran up to close it.

Cheryl was standing in the hallway. "I can't find my purse," she said to him, as if his appearance at her door was both normal and expected. "All my insurance information is in it." She stood there motionless.

Al decided she must be in shock. He walked through the living room, then looked in the kitchen. No purse. He intended to go upstairs but found a woman's black canvas bag at the foot of the staircase. He handed it to her.

"I just have to dig out my keys."

He looked at her shaking hands and commanded, "Don't drive. Come with me."

She obediently followed him to the truck. On the short trip to the hospital she explained what was wrong with Richard. "He was at a day-care center and there was another man there with a bad cold. Richard caught it and then this morning he was having trouble breathing. He looked blue, so I called the rescue squad."

He stood by her while she gave the necessary information to the desk clerk. "We don't have a family doctor," she told the woman apologetically.

Al steered her toward the long wooden bench. Her hair was uncurled and hung in thick straight sheaths. She didn't have on any makeup. Al thought she looked terribly young—a freckled child with invisible eyelashes.

He knew to beware of her, though. At any moment she might realize this wasn't a crisis and remember what he had done to her mother. He tried to steel himself for it.

She stared down at her red sandals. "My feet are dirty," she said softly. "I was up all night with Richard and never got to shower this morning." She snapped her fingers. "I bet this is how it happens. One day you're middle-class and respectable, then something happens. The next day you're in the emergency room and you're dirty and downtrodden." She smiled sadly.

"He's going to be all right."

"I sure hope so. We had an awful fight. Awful. And we really haven't been able to talk since. He doesn't even know I'm pregnant."

He didn't respond to her confidences. Sometime she was going to emerge from her shock, remember who he was, and hate him for knowing these secrets. If he didn't acknowledge hearing them, perhaps she would hate him less.

He studied her profile. Lately she had become pretty. Not beautiful like her mother, but still pretty. She had lost her pudgy, pouting face. Or maybe he found her more attractive because his opinion of her had changed. He used to think her marrying Richard was not much different from a prospective pet owner buying a parakeet because a dog or cat would be too much trouble. But he had been dead wrong. She put a lot of effort into her marriage and gave every appearance of loving her husband.

A nurse emerged to tell them that Richard was having a chest X-ray. Cheryl shifted restlessly, then turned to

Al. "You don't need to stay. It sounds like it will be a while and I'm better now. I can get a ride. If they send Richard home, I'll ride in the ambulance. If not, I'll grab a cab."

"I want to stay. In a little while we'll go get some lunch."

She patted his shoulder gratefully. "You've been so good to us, Al."

How could she say that after what he had done? Then it hit him like a thunderbolt. She didn't know. But then, why was he so surprised about that? A woman who couldn't admit to plucking her eyebrows every week could hardly be expected to tell her daughter she had been raped.

Chapter Twenty-five

Cheryl patted the dog's silky head. She then let Heinz nuzzle up against the skirt of her new white linen suit. "You're really falling upon hard times when I'm your best friend." She gave the dog's head one final pat, then looked back before opening the screen door. "I'll be back so we can go for a walk," she whispered. "We women have to stick together."

Al was in the kitchen preparing a tomato and garlic concoction. She hadn't wanted him to cook. It was enough that he had moved in with them to care for Richard. But when Al had shown so much excitement over recovering his cooking abilities, she had not interfered in the meal preparations.

"Want a little wine or something?" He gave her a deferential smile, aware that he had made her a guest in her own kitchen.

"Not yet, thanks. I'm going to change first and then take Heinz for a constitutional." In case that sounded like a reproach for Al's paying so little attention to the dog, she added, "I've been sitting all day." She clamped hands on hips and added, "I'm about to get programmer's spread."

After a week of classes she had taken to calling herself a systems analyst. But she didn't feel that exalting her embryonic career was necessary in front of Al, who didn't have one.

Richard had been diagnosed as having severe bronchitis. Cheryl felt Al was equally infirm in some mysterious way and was careful what she said to him.

She trudged up the stairs still carrying her briefcase. She dumped its contents on her yellow bedspread.

During the first day of her class Mr. Zishen, the instructor, had mentioned *capturing data* and she had been frightened, immediately deciding that programming must be difficult as catching butterflies with a net. Then Mr. Zishen had her key data into a terminal and it was no more mysterious than statistical typing. In fact, it was easier.

She understood that charting and coding would demand more of her. Still, the process was more straightforward than anything she had studied in college. She had gone to her freshman literature course terrified of symbols. How could the other students find them? She never could. She must lack the equipment necessary to analyze literature. Age had not helped. Just last month she and Richard had read the same book about a woman whose husband was going insane. "Isn't it clever," Richard remarked, "the way she talks about her husband while all the time she's the one who's going crazy?"

She had opened the book and demanded, "Where does it say that?"

He had given her a sympathetic, almost pitying look. "It was just a feeling I got," he answered with exaggerated casualness.

She sat on her bed and touched her plastic flowcharting template. There was no guesswork here. These symbols were tangible and real. The decision block was shaped like a diamond lying sideways. The terminal (start-stop) symbol had the form of a cold capsule. And the off-page connector reminded her of a Boy Scout's badge.

Cheryl was looking forward to doing her homework. She mentally ticked off the things that needed to be done first: change clothes, walk dog, eat dinner with Al.

She threw on jeans and a tentlike madras blouse bought during her high school days. It occurred to her that maternity clothes weren't going to be an enormous expense. After thirteen years of dieting, she already had clothes in all shapes and sizes.

She led the waiting dog to the schoolyard across the
street. When they got to the football field, she let Heinz
off the leash. The dog streaked away. At first she had begun walking Heinz out of guilt, ashamed of the abomi-
nable way she had treated her in the spring. Now she found
herself looking forward to these nightly outings. Besides,
the fresh air and exercise were good for the baby.

After ten minutes, Heinz dutifully trotted back to her.
Cheryl gave the dog a nod of approval. "You're right.
We'd better go back. Al likes to eat early."

The conversation at meals was awkward. Some nights
it was as difficult as a blind date. Simply to end the silence, they often talked about Richard.

"I thought he did a little better today. He had some
soup around four."

"Good." Cheryl spent very little time with Richard.
Al rarely went out, but when he did, she checked on
Richard and brought him cold drinks. On those occasions
she was reserved and studiedly cheerful, like a substitute
attendant.

Richard had said he did not want to be married to her
anymore. Until he was well enough to reconsider, she
was not going to force herself on him. If Al weren't here,
she would have had no choice, would have had to see to
Richard's every need. That might have ended her marriage. It certainly would have ended her career. She stared
at her little garnet wedding ring and said, perhaps for the
twentieth time, "I'm so grateful you're here, Al. Without
your help, I would have been forced to quit work. We
would have gone under."

He never acknowledged her gratitude. Tonight he stared
over at the half-eaten stuffed shells on her plate. "Is my
cooking too spicy for you?" he asked apologetically.

He was obliquely referring to her pregnancy. She
smiled. "No. I'm in tip-top shape. I can eat anything.
But even with eating for two, this was a huge portion."

He shook his head. "You're under too much stress.
It's not right."

She didn't feel all that stressed. She knew Richard was taking a vacation from marriage. But it had stopped hurting her so much. She wasn't enjoying this limbo situation; but it wasn't all that unpleasant either. Going to school and having a stepfather to take care of things made her feel like a child again. There was something especially sweet about being allowed a second childhood right before becoming a parent.

It couldn't have been all that pleasant for Al, though, acting as a male attendant to Richard and sleeping on the couch every night. Though the lack of privacy didn't seem to bother him. And twice a week he did go somewhere. At first she thought he might be dating someone, because he showered and wore a suit coat. But he was always back in an hour and a half—too soon for a date. She would love to know where it was he went. Could he be visiting Rose? She hoped so. She would like her mother back. They'd always had their differences, but at least they used to converse on the phone every day. If Rose got back together with Al, surely she would give up her hermit ways. Cheryl looked hopefully at Al. "Going out tonight?"

"Thought I might."

"Go for as long as you wish. I'll be here doing my homework."

"Won't be gone long."

It was hopeless trying to extract information from him. Defeated, she got up and spooned up raspberry sherbet. Though Al prepared dinner, dessert was still her department. She always had some. It had been months since she had counted calories. But all those mental computations had left her well prepared for calculating print positions. In fact, this mathematical prowess, along with her typing speed, had given her a slight edge over the rest of the programming class. And she wanted desperately to stay at the top of her class. But every day she could feel the others gaining on her.

Chapter Twenty-six

With Al present, Richard found the task hard to accomplish. He had to get the drawer open, pull the bottle out, and take a healthy swig of the pinkish cough syrup without being noticed. He had been pulling it off for four days, but this afternoon Al heard the door open, whipped around, and caught him with the codeine in his hand.

"What the hell! So that's why you've been so sluggish and sleeping all the time."

Richard gripped the bottle protectively. He needed it. The drug was an escape from a battle he wasn't ready to fight.

"That's a heck of a way to treat your wife."

"I haven't heard you being nominated for husband of the year."

Al lunged forward, grabbed Richard's hand, and tried to pull the bottle from him. It shattered from the pressure of their combined grasp and a mixture of cough syrup and blood spilled on Richard's lap.

"You're cut!"

"I'm okay."

Al ran to the kitchen, then returned and immersed the sticky, bleeding hand in a plastic bowl. "It's okay," he said as Al carefully removed the glass-covered top sheet and dumped it into a paper bag. Startled and frightened, he again repeated "I'm okay" when Al approached with a towel to dry the wounded hand.

"I guess you don't need stitches. But you've got to get

up.'' Al's voice broke pitifully and he took a jagged breath before continuing. ''There's glass still in the bed.''

''Okay.''

Al shoved his wheelchair close to the bed, got one brake locked, and helped him hoist himself into it. Richard watched Al closely. Right now he considered him capable of anything, even tears. What had he said to make him act like this? Something about *husband of the year.* A failed marriage was never a joking matter. He should have known better.

It occurred to him that he was becoming something worse than an invalid; he was becoming a creep. He tried to remember the name of that sniveling, crippled creature in *Wuthering Heights* who was such a pitiful excuse for a man. Linton. Was he becoming a Linton? Probably.

He started out to the kitchen, but his hand hurt and it was hard to propel himself forward. When Al returned to help him, he mumbled, ''I'm really sorry for what I said before.''

''S'okay.'' Al picked up his cigarettes and lighter off the kitchen table but quickly set them down again. The Marine insignia on the lighter, a raised globe, made a metallic thump as it hit the Formica surface.

''You can smoke in front of me. My lungs aren't so fragile anymore.'' He felt he must continue to explain himself if he and Al were going to remain friends. ''Used to be that I'd about die every time I got a cold. Now I'm better before I'm ready to be. I was taking the codeine 'cause I was stalling.'' Until he could forgive Cheryl for her treachery. And he wasn't quite ready yet.

Al picked the ashtray off the stove. It was a flimsy piece of tinfoil that Cheryl had brought home from work.

''It wouldn't matter so much if she weren't pregnant.''

Richard snapped his head up. ''Who?''

''Cheryl.''

A nerve began to jump in his right leg. Al had been living here for a while. Could he and Cheryl have . . . ? Had he been sick that long? He stared at the ashtray and tried to remember the last time he had seen Cheryl smoking. It had been months. He also remembered the day after her mother left when she wouldn't take aspirin. That had been over a month ago, too. Of course, the baby was his. He felt deeply ashamed for thinking otherwise. But why hadn't she told him?

"I'm not the one who should be telling you."

That was for damn sure. Still, he was grateful to know. It put everything in a different light. In one of Cheryl's medical books he had read about all the hormonal changes women went through during pregnancy. Cheryl's sticking him in that day-care center hadn't been malicious at all. No, she had just been scared and sick. The hard knot of hate within him lightened and burst as quietly as a child's soap bubble. He longed to talk to her. But she was in a classroom at Software International and completely unavailable to him.

"How about some lunch?"

"Sounds good." Maybe food would give him strength and help clear his brain. He had a considerable amount of thinking to do.

Al set out an onion, a stalk of celery, and a can of tuna.

"Give me the knife and I'll do the slicing and dicing."

Al plunked the wooden cutting board in front of him and Richard began chopping. The bandage complicated an already difficult job. He was able to chunk the celery; but when he tried to pierce the onion, it slipped off the board and rolled across the floor.

Rather than retrieving it, Al took the board and bounded upstairs with it. Richard heard the smack of a hammer. He shuddered. Al had been acting a little weird for a while. But destroying a harmless cutting board clearly put him in the ranks of the seriously deranged.

The board was still intact. All Al had done was to drive a large nail through it; now he anchored the onion on the nail. "Things won't get away from you anymore," he said proudly.

It was incredible! One simple nail would allow him to chop up the ingredients for stews, pies, hors d'oeuvres. "This is great. You're a genius."

"You and my mother. Take a nail out for her; stick one in for you. And you both think I'm a genius."

Al's eyes watered dangerously and Richard tried to think of something noncommittal to say about the late Mrs. Valerino. "Is the estate settled?"

Al served coffee and sandwiches before answering. "Sort of. She left the house to me." He stirred his coffee but forgot to remove the spoon and now knocked himself in the mouth with every sip. "I thought I ought to sell it and split the money with my brothers. But this counselor I go to says I should keep it. So I thought maybe I'd give the house to Rose as reparation."

The word *counselor* seemed to float ceilingward and hang suspended over the stove long after everything else Al said had evaporated. He pulled a folded sheet of paper from his wallet and handed it to Richard. "This is Rose's number. I know she won't talk to me. But I thought maybe you would talk to her and see if she'd like the house. The apartment house she's living in looks like a real dump."

Richard set the number to the left of his place mat.

He found the number in the morning and remembered he had promised to call. It wasn't an assignment that worried him. Solving Al's marital problems would be far easier than solving his own. What had happened to them was very clear. Al in the throes of a mid-life crisis had had an affair with a younger woman—maybe not even an affair. Probably just an infatuation. Whatever, it was over and now he wanted his wife back.

Solving that would be a piece of cake. He would just explain to Rose that Mrs. Valerino's death had precipitated some kind of emotional crisis in Al. But what would he do about Cheryl? She had obviously slipped out to

work early without waking him to say goodbye. How long
could they live like this?

There wasn't even anyone to discuss it with because
Al had moved home last night. He drank two cups of
coffee, then slowly read the newspaper, going through
the want ads with more care than ever before. If he and
Cheryl were truly going to have a baby, he would have
to find a way to make some money. With summer over,
the columns were getting smaller and smaller. He was
hoping for something like telephone sales from the home.
But the only listings in that entire alphabetical section
were for a shampoo assistant and a tire changer.

It was hopeless. After lunch he pulled out Cheryl's
Fannie Farmer Cookbook and looked for an interesting
way to prepare the chicken defrosting in the refrigerator.
Paella! He had all the ingredients.

The freezer contained both frozen shrimp and peas.
Cook; remove; set aside. That had to be done at least
four times before combining the ingredients in a large
casserole. It was the perfect recipe to occupy his afternoon. He got out the cutting board and began to slice—
first an onion and then a pepper. Later he cooked the
rice.

He hadn't expected this meal to save his marriage. The
way to a woman's heart is not through her stomach. But
he thought Cheryl might have appreciated the effort he
went to.

She ate lightly, politely sampling everything. She
would have done the same if he had served sawdust. Al's
abrupt departure had frightened her. "Damn it, Cheryl,"
he wanted to scream, "we don't need a chaperone. We're
married." But he did not raise his voice; he had to be
gentle with her. Besides, after reading all those romantic
novels, something in this strained situation might appeal
to her. Half the time, those heroes and heroines were
already married but living as strangers because of some
grievous mutual misunderstanding.

He personally could find nothing romantic in this awkward silence and decided there were times when the only way to get someone's attention was to resort to gossip. And if that someone was the woman you love, you will even sacrifice your best friend. To stay spiritually pure, one had to be willing to remain unloved and alone. Now he knew why priests and nuns were forbidden to marry.

"Al is seeing a counselor."

"He's what?" Cheryl shifted her attention from her plate to him. "Why?"

"I don't know why. But he's going—two nights a week. That's what he told me."

"So that's where he went. He'd get dressed and go out. At first I thought he might be going to see my mother. But then he asked me where she was living."

He was relieved to hear her voice soften and lose the hard, defensive edge she had spoken with earlier. Sure, she was hurt. But they would hash it out this evening. Make some resolutions so nothing like this could ever happen again. After that she would tell him about the baby.

"How did the class go today?"

She frowned ferociously. "I had a loop in a program. If my teacher hadn't caught it, it would still be running. I've got to be more careful and study harder. I used to think I was in the running to be in the top of my class. But it's impossible."

She looked so disappointed. Why wasn't she equally disappointed about their marriage? It wasn't the time for complaints. His job was to be gentle. "Why is it so important to be at the top of the class?"

"The top three in my class get to interview with Paul Birch, the design genius. I've heard his voice on the phone. But to meet him as a peer and have a shot at a really interesting job instead of just doing maintenance programming all my life would make all the difference."

She had gotten so ambitious so fast. It was hard to understand how a discontented secretary could find maintenance programming, whatever that was, not challenging enough. "If you want it badly enough, you can still come out on top."

She shook her head sadly. "Most of these people have already had data processing courses. Some even worked on the big T.I.C. Project #5 in the V.S. conversion."

He didn't know what she was talking about, only that it was terribly important to her. He was going to have to be patient. Surely some sleepless night she would realize that an IBM/370 mainframe was not a direct link to God. In the meantime if she needed and wanted to be first-string, he was going to help her make it. He owed her that. "You can beat them. There's a lot to be said for natural ability and for just wanting it so much that it makes your teeth ache. Those kids who played peewee football are always burnt out by the time they get to college."

"I guess so." She sounded far from convinced.

After they finished their coffee Cheryl picked up her briefcase and said apologetically, "All those years when I was a secretary I really wanted to carry a briefcase and look important. I never thought about what it really meant. I have a bunch of homework to do."

Homework? It was Friday night.

She appeared to read his mind. "I've also got to go in tomorrow and run a couple of programs. Turnaround is so much better on the weekends."

"Sure. I understand."

"Do you need help with anything down here?"

He shook his head vigorously.

"Then, I'll see you in the morning."

It was going to take a little longer than he had planned. Still, he had lots of time.

Too much time. The evening stretched ahead interminably, and he was glad the bottle of cough syrup was broken. Recovering from drug dependency must be close to impossible. When you were powerless and things turned out wrong, the urge to tune out was pretty strong. Cheryl used to do it with food. He hadn't noticed her sneaking off with cookies lately. Her job was making her feel special and important—a state she hadn't known since her father's death.

His own ego wasn't that dependent on work, which was a darn good thing. He had always known he had a certain power over other people—charisma, whatever. When he got into trouble was when he ceased to care about the people. But that wasn't going to happen anymore. Together, he and Cheryl had created someone new, someone independent who was going to be dependent on them for a couple of decades. It changed the whole ballgame. Not *it*, he chided himself. The baby, the baby.

The baby was going to change his life, and so was Cheryl's career. If she was going to remain so involved in her work, he was going to have to find something of his own to get into.

After finishing the dishes he got a yellow-lined pad to make a list of possible occupations. Nothing came to mind. He was an English major turned football player. Besides, transportation was a big problem. How would he get to a job?

1. WRITE A BOOK.

What kind of book would he write? What did he know to write about? Certainly not other people. He barely spoke to other people anymore.

1. WRITE A BOOK.
   A) *Autobiography*

I started playing football to prove I wasn't a coward. Let me explain that. Bear with me. I've got to backtrack.

One night when I was nine my grandma and I were staring out the window of our eighth-floor apartment window. It was one of those steamy Florida nights when you smell a combination of jasmine and smoke from those fires always burning in the Everglades.

*A man in yellow slacks got out of a fish-tailed Cadillac.
Something about Florida makes women lose their modesty and men lose their manhood. You see sagging wrinkled women walk down the street with their bathing suits all hiked up in the rear. Right behind them are the men in pink slacks and white knit shirts, all gone to blubber. This guy was like that, jowly with a big bloated stomach pushing against the polyester pants and white stretch belt. He got out of the car. Then he neatly and quietly keeled over.*

The medics came, ripped off his shirt, and pushed on him. When that didn't work, they put these cymbals to his chest, which caused him to convulse like a fish still on the hook.

Right then and there my grandma made me promise—cross my heart and hope to die—that if she was dying nice and clean from a heart attack not to call the rescue squad.

She didn't get up one morning during my sophomore year in high school. When I went to her bedroom she was ashen and kept pointing to her mouth. I brought her a Dixie cup of water. She didn't want it. Next I brought her husband's picture. I was a romantic and thought maybe she wanted to kiss it or something.

She still kept pointing to her mouth. Finally I brought the false teeth that were in a plastic cup on her dresser. She patted my hand gratefully. Right after that she died.

The doctor told my mom that Grandma could have been saved if I had been calm enough to call the rescue squad. Word got out that I was a coward.

What crap! Richard read what he had written, then tore it up and slammed it into the wastebasket. A private trust was a private trust—even if one party was dead and the other was broke and lonely. There wasn't going to be any book.

To pass the time, he looked through some of Cheryl's magazines and copied recipes he thought they both might like. At least he could keep up his share of the cooking and housework. The cutting board Al fixed was going to be a big help.

And there was some progress with his mobility. Every day he practiced walking, and lately his left leg had shown a little improvement. It still felt stiff and rusty. But he was going to walk again. He knew it for a fact. He would tell Cheryl when she told him her news.

In the morning he fixed Cheryl a sandwich with the leftover tuna from the lunch Al had fixed, then perked a big pot of coffee so she could take a thermos with her.

"There's a coffee machine at the office," she said. But she quickly regretted her lack of gratitude. "But this will be much better."

Halfway to the door, she turned and asked shyly, "Have you got anything to do today?"

Sure, he had plans. First he intended to take an inventory of the refrigerator and cupboards and make up a grocery list. Then he planned to go through the rest of the magazines for recipes, copy them for future reference, and pick one to have for dinner tonight.

It was going to be a full and busy day. But that sounded too pathetic to tell her. "I've started writing a book. I guess I'll work on that."

The refrigerator contained four different kinds of cheeses, two half-full bottles of wine, and very little else. Finding a recipe required some ingenuity. In the cupboard were canned goods, cereal, and noodles. He looked through two cookbooks, then started reading women's magazines. In an issue of *New Woman* he came across an article on making it big at the office.

The author suggested the ambitious woman master football strategy and jargon so she could understand how to act in a male-dominated corporation. Well, if Cheryl needed any help in that area, she'd married the right man. He wished she'd start talking about the people in her class, instead of the computer equipment. Next he saw a

picture of MacLogan Ross modeling a dress that looked
like a man's shirt. Poor Logan! She wasn't aging well.

Finally in *Complete Woman*, he found a recipe for
spinach noodle casserole:

> 8 oz. spinach macaroni, cooked
> ³/₄ cup chopped onion
> 1 can of cream of mushroom soup,
>   diluted with ¹/₂ can of milk
> ¹/₄ tsp. paprika
> 8 oz. swiss cheese, sliced
> ¹/₃ cup buttered bread crumbs
>   Salt and pepper to taste.

He skipped the salt. He had heard it was bad for pregnant women. He served the casserole with three-bean
salad. He gave Cheryl a big glass of water. In his morning reading he had also discovered the importance of
fluids during pregnancy.

No matter what place mats he used, the dinner still
looked poverty-stricken. Rather than apologize, he told
Cheryl, "Al's going to take me to the grocery store tomorrow. I think with careful shopping I can get groceries
that will last us for about three weeks. You'll only have
to stop for milk and stuff like that."

"Okay."

"I'm going to probably use most of my Social Security
check for groceries." He had never made any claim on
this money before and was anxious for her reaction. She
just nodded absently. It was obvious she had something
else on her mind.

After eating two of the canned peaches he served for
dessert, she set down her spoon abruptly. "There's
something I've got to tell you. I hope you're not upset."

His heart constricted and he steeled himself to hear
about the baby that almost was. He couldn't blame her.
With a sick husband and a brand-new job most women
would consider abortion.

"I called the sports editor at the *Ridgely Journal* and told him you were writing a book. He was amazed you weren't in a hospital and said that there was a story just in that. He said he was going to talk to the lifestyles editor on Monday and she would probably call you sometime next week."

She found these newspaper types' interest encouraging. She didn't know they never turned down a story idea. Filling all that space day after day got to be such a nuisance that at times they would write an article about almost anything.

"What kind of book are you writing? I felt stupid when he asked and I didn't know."

His only attempt at composition had ended up in the garbage can. He stared over at the lined pad that now contained only recipes. "A cookbook." One lie was never enough. He had to add: "A special cookbook for one-handed cooks." He showed her the nail Al had driven through the cutting board. Once he started he couldn't stop embellishing. "I'm going to call around to some occupational therapists and get some other tips."

She shook her head. "I'm surprised. I was sure it would be an autobiography and then I'd have to read about all your old flames."

Her eyes began to tear. He knew what a strain she had been under these last few weeks. "Cheryl, I'm sorry. I'm so sorry."

She reached out her hand and he took it. He was glad her recent weight loss had not changed the shape of her fingers. They were still womanly, generous, and looked the same as that day in the nursing home when she had handed him the pink Kleenex.

Tonight the stakes were nearly as high as the day when he had asked her to marry him. "Please," he implored, trying unsuccessfully to keep his voice from breaking, "don't go upstairs tonight."

"No, I won't. But you have to promise me not to give up and get sick when things go wrong next time."

"No, next time I'll stick around and we'll work out a compromise."

They went to bed early and were tender and shy with each other. But she did not tell him about the baby and now he knew she never would. His lack of support had forced her to do the unthinkable. Now they could not even discuss the worst loss in their young lives. He slowly ran his fingers through her hair. They would live through fall and winter grieving in their own ways. But by spring they would begin to heal. He took her hand and gently pressed it to his lips.

In the morning he wanted to wake up slowly, then drink coffee and have a leisurely breakfast. But Cheryl had become a churchgoer. She got up early to prepare for Mass. He wasn't surprised to see her leave wearing the lime-green dress she had married him in. For some inexplicable reason, she had begun to wear that dress frequently.

While she was out he started to cook breakfast. He fried the bacon until the strips turned translucent. He would restart the burner right before she was due home. He pulled Bisquick from the shelf and mixed up the batter for biscuits. It was a cool enough morning not to mind turning on the oven.

He thought the hot biscuits, appetizing-looking bowl of fruit cocktail, and the smell of cooking bacon would please her. Instead, she paled perceptibly and rushed past him toward the sliding patio door. Once it was opened, she began to gulp the crisp air greedily.

Richard had not rehearsed anything to do or say because he thought it was too late. He shut off the burner and lifted a ten-pound bag of sugar from the storage shelf, then followed her over by the door. When she turned, he balanced the sugar on his upper chest and began to pat it rhythmically.

She shook her head gravely. "Babies don't stay that still." She stared at him intently. "I thought you knew. Does it show?"

"Your hands," he said impulsively.

It appeared to have been the right answer. She nodded, lifted her hands with palms facing him, and said, "Sure, swollen and pink. They're a dead giveaway."

He jiggled the sack of sugar on his knee and then stood and walked carefully to the coffee table. He set the sugar down gently and proceeded to cover it with an imaginary blanket.

"You've really made progress with the walking. I had no idea."

Of course she had no idea. It had been very hard to command her attention lately. But there was no resentment in his reply. "It's going to be okay," he said with the confidence that had once been his trademark. "We're going to be able to take care of this baby."

Chapter Twenty-seven

There were three of them waiting to see Paul Birch. The secretary had ushered them into an office-size waiting room with gray velour chairs. Cheryl picked a *Datamation Magazine* off the glass-topped coffee table and began to lazily leaf through it.

She could sense the nervousness of the two young men waiting with her. It was too bad they were getting so worked up over this interview. She had been at Software International long enough to know that Paul Birch wasn't going to hire any of them. He always talked to the top three graduates from the data processing course; in the last three years, though, he had never hired them. He was looking for some rare type of genius; none of them fit the bill.

She sneaked a glance at Charlie, the younger of her two companions. The baby-faced twenty-two-year-old had a scared smile plastered on his face and was too nervous even to pretend to read. Cheryl had known him before their course. A plodder, he had worked his way up from the mailroom through hard work and night courses. Now he had finished third in the data processing course out of a class of thirty—an honor Software International would not overlook. But he wouldn't get in the design department. Even the spiffy three-piece suit he was wearing wouldn't help. Birch didn't have room for plodders.

Steve, a slight, mustached blond, had a slightly better chance. He had an honors degree from a Florida college

196

and a master's in information science. He was presentable enough, but there was something about him Cheryl didn't like. She watched him reading intently as if he expected even now to glean some information useful to him in his upcoming interview. Cheryl realized why she did not like him: he was a user. Every pleasantry she had ever uttered to him he had probably filed away in memory to use again for the betterment of his own career. He was also very competitive. When he hadn't been able to read her test scores by leaning toward her in a mockingly sexual way, he had out and out asked.

The secretary quietly came in. "Mr. Birch is tied up with a client. He suggests you all go out to lunch and"— the elegantly dressed woman checked her watch—"come back about 2:30."

Cheryl gave the secretary a radiant smile. She appreciated the woman's tact. Birch, she was positive, had said nothing about lunch. When reminded there were candidates to interview, he had probably snarled, "Get rid of them until 2:30."

Charlie, still smiling, shrugged. "We're getting paid to sit here."

Steve Elden was less easygoing about the delay. He stood up rigidly, clenching and unclenching his fists. "Birch is," he mumbled, "playing games with us. He wants to maintain the pressure a little longer—see how we hold up."

Cheryl shook her head. "Na. He just got busy with a client. He hasn't got time for games. Let's go to lunch."

"You know him?" Elden gave her an interested smile.

To think she used to fall in love with guys that were this obvious! Now he was going to pump her all through lunch about Birch. The creep! "My former boss marketed a lot of his software packages. I don't know him personally."

Birch's secretary was standing outside the waiting room door and must have heard Elden's outburst. She gave no evidence of it, though. "See you at 2:30," she said politely.

Cheryl nodded. "We'll be here. Thank you."

They decided to eat at Grateful Fridays, a Software International hangout with hanging plants, huge windows, and butcher block tables. The high-backed chairs were terribly uncomfortable. Cheryl thought their selection had been intentional. The place had a huge lunch and dinner crowd and didn't take kindly to lingerers. No matter how she shifted, her back still felt unsupported. Finally she just gave up, leaned forward, and studied the menu.

A cheerful young waitress approached them. "How about something from the bar?"

Charlie, who had never quite lost his nervous smile, now openly grinned back. "I'll have a vodka tonic." Then he flushed, embarrassed to have ordered before Cheryl.

She shook her head. "I'm not ready yet." She finished reading the list of special summer drinks. *Banana blitz— a tackling combo of bananas, rum, and triple sec. Strawberry fizz—a foot-high cooler of fresh strawberries, vanilla ice cream, rum, and grenadine.*

Steve ordered tonic and lime. Cheryl sensed Charlie's discomfort. He had blundered again. A sensible jobseeker did not drink before an interview. But only if you had a chance at getting the job, Cheryl thought—and ordered a white wine spritzer. She knew she shouldn't be drinking much, but surely diluted wine wouldn't hurt the baby. It had to be preferable to a banana blitz.

"So what's Birch like?" Elden asked nonchalantly. He had tried to wait a decent interval before introducing the only subject that interested him.

"Young, I think," she answered before taking a sip of her spritzer. "He's rumored to be quite a tyrant to his people. Makes them wear beepers so he knows where they are at all times. I've heard he only wants yes-men."

Nothing could have been further from the truth. Cheryl

knew secretaries in the design department who had developed all sorts of stress-related ailments because Birch gave his people such a free rein. On a typical morning an analyst might phone in saying "I've been working on the ADP program all night. I'm going to grab some sleep and be in later." She could sympathize with the secretaries. How did you answer the phone for a man who was grabbing sleep on company time? She anxiously looked at Charlie to see if he would contradict her false portrayal of Birch. But he was busy eating french fries and had no apparent interest in their conversation. Mailroom employees might not be as interested in the executives' personalities as secretaries were.

She removed her mushroom burger from its roll and began to chop it up into tiny bite-size pieces.

"Someone's waving at you," Charlie told her.

Cheryl looked up and there on the level above them was Lucy, leaning against the ledge and waving madly.

"Friend of yours? Single?"

Poor Charlie. He went to night school, lived in a studio apartment, and during their class had never mentioned having a date.

"Yeah. I'll introduce you sometime."

"Thanks."

"You're awfully calm and casual about this."

Cheryl didn't know if Elden was referring to her manner or her dress. In case it was the latter, she said, "I guess I should have worn a suit, but this is a lot more comfortable." She had worn the lime wedding dress because it had an elastic waist. "I'm to the point of pregnancy where my clothes fit a bit funny."

She took in his expression: relief. He no longer considered her a competitor. "Bad timing," he said sympathetically.

"There's no bad time for babies. Congratulations."

"Thanks, Charlie." She would have to introduce him to Lucy. They both had a romantic way of viewing things.

It was not quite 2:30 when they returned, but this time

Birch was waiting for them. The secretary escorted Charlie in first.

Cheryl picked up the same magazine and began to flip through its pages. She felt slighted at the high-handedness. She was the only woman: Paul Birch should have talked to her first. *There you go again*, she scolded herself, *finding insult where none was intended.*

She remembered an anecdote someone had once told her about Birch. Supposedly he and one of his female analysts were walking down the hall talking. She stepped into the ladies' room and he, intent on their conversation and oblivious of the gender difference, had walked right in with her. Well, that was probably a huge exaggeration. But still, he probably did not adhere to the ladies-first adage.

The secretary again appeared. "Mr. Elden."

Cheryl slid back in her chair and got comfortable. Steven Elden would take a while.

But he didn't. The secretary was back almost immediately to summon Cheryl, then lead her down the short hallway to the end office. *Calm down*, she warned herself. *This is just an exercise. Nothing will come of it.* But her body refused to listen and remained on red alert.

He was young! Really young—maybe just a year or two older than herself. There wasn't even a hint of gray in his dark hair. She had expected him to be about forty. At Software that was young.

He shook her hand and motioned her to the visitor's chair. There was a coffeepot on his credenza. "Like a cup?"

She knew better than to accept a cup at the hairdresser because it just got in the way. But now she heard herself saying "That would be nice."

He served them both. "Why did you drop out of college?" he asked, settling into his own chair.

Interviews weren't supposed to start like this! That magazine for female executives she used to subscribe to always advised chatting until the candidate was relaxed and comfortable. No wonder Elden was out of here in record time. She probably wouldn't even have a chance to taste her coffee. She had been foolish to accept it. "I didn't find anything there that I loved to do or was especially good at."

"Did you ever find anything you loved doing?"

She had regretted saying *love* instead of like. But when he repeated it, the word sounded strong and appropriate. "Just last month. When I got into that class, it was like a fish discovering water."

He half smiled, but the intensity of his questions didn't lessen. "But you *were* a good secretary?"

"I was responsible, dependable, all that. But I always resented the job."

"Why?" He regarded her seriously.

Before Richard, his rapt attention would have sent her into a frenzy. She would have spent the entire interview speculating on his marital status. But guys like Birch gave the best part of themselves to their jobs. She would love to work with him; she had no desire to marry him.

"Because I hated being invisible. Delivering coffee at meetings, but having to keep my opinions to myself."

"Did you?"

"Keep my opinions to myself? Yes, I did."

"My secretary never does. She scheduled you to come in last because she said you were the only one worth spending time with." He grinned mischievously. "But I must admit I was intrigued by you before that. You go into that class with absolutely no prior training and come out number one. Sixty percent of that class had already taken courses in a specific language. The bozo that was just in here ahead of you graduated magna cum laude with a B.S. in computer science and had a master's degree in something or other. And you beat him, too."

Her face flushed; her hands grew cold. It was just too cruel to think about—she almost had a chance to join the design group. Damn! Why did her luck run this way? Stop, she warned herself. You will still get a job. Nothing flashy or fun like working here. Probably it would be an applications job maintaining the payroll system. Still, she should be grateful and not think about what might have been.

"You are going to have to take some math courses."

"I'm pregnant, Mr. Birch."

That stunned him. He rested his head on his arm. She thought he looked almost disappointed. "What will that entail—the pregnancy?"

He was just being polite; he couldn't really care. "Six weeks off in about six months."

She could almost hear Richard prompting her: "Go for it. Go for it."

She really didn't have anything to lose. "My husband works at home, so I won't have any child-care problems."

He was staring morosely out the window. She wasn't sure if he had heard her. Perhaps she should just politely mumble "I'm sorry to have taken your time" and go.

"What's he do?" He had been so still, it startled her when he spoke.

"He's a writer." It wasn't a lie. It was just what Richard called being positive: describe everything as favorably as possible. When in a pinch, exaggerate. It would probably happen anyway.

Birch locked his knuckles, continued staring out the window. His behavior frightened her. Maybe she shouldn't care about not getting this job. Would she even want to work for someone who would suddenly become so remote and cold?

He swiveled around to face her. "I appreciate your honesty. I wanted to hire you. It's good for all of us to have somebody fresh and excited join us. Training someone keeps us in touch with the basics. But the math—you are going to have to take it sometime. Maybe we can find you a class during the day?"

"I could go to the class on my lunch hour." She wished she could say, "Oh, this is an easy pregnancy. I could take a night course." But it would have been a lie. Already she was in bed by ten. Think what another three months would bring!

He shook his head again, troubled, and she was sure he was going to tell her he was sorry. . . .

He scribbled something on a memo sheet and shoved it at her. "Personnel will make you a formal offer. But this is the salary. I'm sorry, but knowing what you told me, I've got to bring you in as a level 5 trainee because your training program will take longer. We'll have you writing out program documentation and matters like that at first. It's no executive position."

She stared at what he had scribbled on the paper. It was seven thousand more than she was currently making. "This would be fine."

"Are you sure? You can't change your mind three months from now. I've heard writers don't make a lot of money."

"I'm thrilled with this. My husband will be, too."

"One last thing. I expect all my people to do a great job, so I don't pat heads or give out compliments. Your monthly check is our expression of appreciation."

"I'll remember that." They solemnly shook hands, and he reverted to his window-staring.

She let herself out, gave his secretary a grateful wave, and started down the hall. She had a new job ahead of her and so did Richard. If Birch never gave out compliments, then Richard was going to have to buck her up even more than he did already.

Chapter Twenty-eight

Rose was sweating from the exertion of having just walked up the steep hill on Lincoln Avenue. She was also afraid. Gas stations had always terrified her. They were dark foreign places with a language she didn't understand.

She stood humbly by the service counter for some time before a long-haired boy in a greasy sweatshirt approached and mumbled, "Help you?"

She pointed back in the direction of the hill. "My car died on Lincoln Avenue."

"The make of the deceased?"

She ignored his mocking smile and said severely, "It's a blue 1983 Buick Skylark."

"Is it blocking traffic?"

"No. I was able to get it off the street. If I floor it, it will jerk a couple of feet forward. But that's it." She set her keys down on the counter, then gave him her name and address.

"The tow truck is out. We'll get you next. But the mechanic won't have time to look at it until sometime Monday."

Two more days without a car! She hadn't bought groceries yet. How was she going to get to church tomorrow and her summer school class on Monday? "All right," she said wearily, and started on the long walk home.

Though it was unseasonably warm, she kept her trench coat tightly belted. Garages and mechanics always made her feel exposed and vulnerable. It was so obvious when you didn't have a man living with you. One look under your hood and your solitary state was totally apparent. The fan belts would be frayed and the radiator dry—because women had never been taught to fathom these mysteries.

Rose remembered her relief yesterday at walking into a hardware store almost completely staffed by women. A brunette in bib overalls had been able to explain how to fix the broken chain on a toilet with straightforward delicacy. Someday Ridgely would have female mechanics, though probably not in her lifetime.

She stepped up her pace as she approached her own neighborhood. It was a poor area with run-down homes inhabited by three and four families. The house on the corner was the worst. Used tires piled up like a platter of doughnuts stood by the back door. An abandoned washing machine, rusting in the sun, occupied a prominent space midyard, as if it were a suitable substitute for a birdbath or some other lawn ornament.

And today, as always, the front yard was full of half-dressed children and beer-drinking men. She walked by quickly with her head down. She hoped no one in the group would shout or stare at her. Her heart pounded and her side hurt, but she didn't slow until she reached the rickety stairs leading to her own walk-up. Soon she would move. After a few more paychecks had accumulated in her checking account—*if* the car didn't cost too much to fix.

Her front door was plywood-thin and had been slightly warped from either weather or a forced entry. Rose thought it might have been the latter, so she had had a chain lock installed at her own expense. It hadn't made her feel much safer. Every little noise made her start. And last night a group of boys selling candy bars to benefit the athletic program had completely terrified her.

She had already been in bed when they had pounded on her door. She had remained there in a terrified huddle until their knocking stopped. Then she had peered out the window and seen them there with their innocent candy bars.

Rose had adopted the habit of going to bed at 8 P.M. For three hours she slept peacefully. Then at eleven she automatically woke and was unable to relax and return to sleep until around four. She felt that if the apartment was going to be burglarized it would happen between eleven and four.

It was so silly. She told herself that daily. There was nothing to be afraid of. She didn't own any expensive jewelry or irreplaceable artifacts. She had already been raped. Still, she could not kid herself into a sense of security. What had happened with Al was child's play compared with what could happen with a stranger. She was going to stay vigilant.

Rose shed her raincoat and checked the refrigerator. Dinner was going to be simple: an English muffin, a cup of instant soup, and an orange. She placed her meager dinner on a tray and carried it into the living room. Eating with the evening news had become a habit. Though she knew listening to the nightly recitation of violent acts did nothing to calm her or aid digestion. She set the tray on the coffee table, carefully avoiding the newspaper section resting there. She had saved last Sunday's local supplement because her daughter and son-in-law beamed at the world from a color photograph on the cover.

According to the article, Richard was writing a book, and Cheryl had found herself a wonderful job. She had sent them a congratulatory card. Greeting cards were exemplary because they placed no burden on the recipient. Cheryl and Richard now had her address; if they felt like getting in touch, they could; if they didn't, they were under no pressure or obligation to do so.

She washed her dishes, watched two situation comedies, and got ready for bed. There wasn't any milk left, but she found herself feeling quite sleepy without it. Relieved the active part of the day was over, she pulled on her nightgown, and got into bed.

The bedside princess phone woke her with loud, shrill peals.

"How are you, Rose?" came a vaguely familiar voice.

She remembered the mocking smile of the gas station attendant and was afraid to speak.

"It's Richard," the phone voice said urgently. "Are you all right?"

"Oh. I must have fallen asleep in front of the television." She looked at the little clock on her nightstand. It wasn't quite nine. She couldn't admit to being in bed. "I read about you in the newspaper."

"We got your card. Thank you. You know *The New York Times* picked up the story. Since then, three publishing houses have offered to give me an advance on the cookbook."

"That's wonderful."

"Incredible. That people remember me. But I'm not so sure I want them to. Even so, the manuscript is keeping me busy. I'm going to interview some agents and there's an occupational therapist in New Milford who wants to collaborate with me. But," he added in a rush, "that's not why I called."

"Yes?" She was glad he hadn't changed, was still boyish and affectionate.

"Well, I've always believed in minding my own business. . . ."

She had never known Richard to be hesitant or find a subject awkward. Was it something with Cheryl? "But you're going to meddle now, right?" she said in what she hoped was a playful tone.

"Yes, 'cause I know what happened to you and Al."

She choked, then fought for air. This was the greatest humiliation yet—that her daughter and son-in-law knew. She couldn't bear it.

"So he had a fling with some young girl after his mother died. It didn't mean anything. He's been going to pieces ever since you left him. And it certainly shouldn't keep you away from Cheryl and me."

Rose felt relief. Or was it anger? He's been going to pieces ever since I left him? Why is his welfare my responsibility? I'm going to pieces myself. Nobody is blaming him. It wasn't Richard's fault. He didn't know any better. "I needed time," she said gently.

"Sure. Of course. But we miss you."

Did *we* include Cheryl? She had run away leaving all those unplanted flowers. Could Cheryl forgive something like that? She doubted it.

"We're having a few people over tomorrow—the secretary who replaced Cheryl and a guy from her programming class. Why don't you join us?"

If it were Cheryl issuing the invitation, Rose would have walked the full six miles to their home. But Richard might be forcing an encounter here that Cheryl didn't even know about. "My car is in the garage until at least Monday. Besides, I'd rather visit when you don't have other guests. It's been a long time since I've seen Cheryl."

"Okay. How about dinner on Thursday?"

"Won't that be hard with her working?"

"No. Richard is doing all the cooking and testing his recipes. I lead a charmed life."

Cheryl was on the kitchen extension! Her daughter wanted her. "I'd love to come over. I want to hear all about your new job."

"Good. I've got some other things to tell you about, too."

There was a gentle click. Cheryl had hung up. Richard cleared his throat, and Rose realized that he hadn't yet approached the subject he found awkward.

"One other thing. Al was left his mother's home. He asked me to ask you if you'd like to live there."

"Tell him no, thank you."

"Wait a minute. This shrink he is seeing—"

A shrink! He was blurting out all his troubles to a psychiatrist when he hadn't been able to tell her what color tie he'd prefer? Her neck began to stiffen. "Is this doctor a man or a woman?'' She had to know that. If it was a woman, it would mean their marriage was a total sham. It would prove he could talk to women, just not to her.

"I don't know. You can ask him. I told him to stop by your place around noon tomorrow and explain this house deal.''

"Did you invite him for lunch, too?'' she asked testily.

"No. He won't stay long.''

It was impossible to offend Richard. He always believed in the rightness of what he did.

Rose slammed the phone down, then slipped her feet into terrycloth scuffs and went out to the kitchen. There was nothing to eat. She put the teakettle on and got out a package of Saltines. She had no intention of seeing Al. It wasn't Richard's fault; he didn't know what had happened. But his ignorance did not obligate her to being home at noon.

She slathered peanut butter on the crackers and made plans. She would leave the house at eleven and slowly walk to noon Mass. She had no intention of remaining home cowering behind a locked door all day.

Rose stopped at a McDonald's after Mass, though she knew it wasn't necessary. Al wasn't a patient man. He could never wait for anything. On their honeymoon trip to Disney World, they had walked from exhibit to exhibit and seen nothing but the evening fireworks because he refused to wait in line.

Waiting must have made him feel powerless. Had that restlessness been a sign that he was dangerous? If it was, she had never picked up on it. She had always felt safe with Al. He let her make the decisions. It was so different from her first marriage where George always had the upper hand. He had never consulted her on anything—cars, vacations, gifts for Cheryl.

But maybe George's way was better. She had certainly paid dearly for being the leading partner; it was obviously a luxury women couldn't afford. After finishing her giant iced tea, she decided to buy herself a second cheeseburger. There was nothing at home to eat but peanut butter.

It was close to three that afternoon when she passed the ramshackle house on the corner. The disorder seemed more of an eyesore on Sundays. Her mother had felt hanging out wash on the Sabbath was a sacrilege. What would she think about these aimless, bloated men and popsicle-stained children who flaunted their poverty.

Al had been seated on the bottom step, but when he saw her approaching, he stood.

Rose did not notice him until he moved. He had on a suit she had never seen before. His face was flushed and mournful. He raised his hand in a timid half wave, which she did not return. He was the conqueror. What right did he have to look so beaten?

When she was within hearing range, he said, "I know you don't want to see me. But I have to tell you how sorry I am." He pulled a document of some kind from his pocket. "I want you to have this."

Rose shook her head. Her calves ached from just having walked four miles—a useless effort. She invited him in because he obviously didn't expect to be allowed in and because she did not want to have such a personal conversation in the street.

He was shocked by the poverty of her surroundings. She watched him take in the garish pink cabinets, the shabby furniture, and the cigarette-burned rug.

"I'll make us some tea." She needed to give this visit some structure but was afraid he would come into the kitchen entryway and watch her while she filled the teakettle and pulled down cups. But he didn't. He stayed seated precariously on the living room couch, not even presumptuous enough to remove his suit coat.

He reminded her of college boys she had dated. They were so polite and formal on the first few dates. But in an amazingly short time they became authoritarian and demanding. She pulled two tea bags out of the cabinet.

I wasn't made for intimacy, she told herself. I should never have married. Well, she had been punished. Her first husband had been cheerfully and continuously unfaithful. Now she was politely making tea for a man who had killed her with silence, then raped her. Her eyes watered and her hands fumbled to locate the mugs.

They were cheap plastic. One thumped on the floor, but was incapable of breaking.

Hearing the commotion, Al had moved to the doorway. "Can I help?"

"No." Desperate for something to say, she pointed to the pink cabinets beside her. "Awful color."

"I could sand and repaint them for you."

She shook her head vigorously, but could not check the flow of tears. How humiliating it was to continue loving a man who had deliberately harmed you.

He moved forward slowly, as if land mines were hidden in the space between them. He touched her shoulder tentatively with his fingertips. Detecting no resistance, he grasped her firmly while softly repeating, "There, there. There, there."

Epilogue

When Richard's book was published a year later, the dedication read:

> In gratitude to Cheryl, Rose, and Al.
> And a special thank-you to my daughter,
> Sara, for taking long afternoon naps.

THIRD PRINTING!
NOW AT YOUR BOOKSTORE!

SKILLET EASE

by

Richard
Olsen

A COOKBOOK FOR THE KITCHEN-SHY

With an introduction by Marcia Thompson, O.P.T.

"A tantalizing collection of nourishing skillet meals
. . . Easy-to-read, easy-to-follow recipes."
—*The Boston Globe*

NIALL LUHRS PRESS

About the Author

In 1984 Kathleen O'Connor took first prize for fiction in the Connecticut National Writing Awards. She was also a recipient of the James Michener Fellowship at the Iowa Writers' Workshop. Ms. O'Connor's short fiction has appeared in national magazines. *The Way It Happens in Novels* is her first novel.